THE ...
L ... E

Barbara Cartland

Barbara Cartland Ebooks Ltd

This edition © 2015

ISBNs

9781782136897   EPUB

978-1517277628   PAPERBACK

Book design by M-Y Books
m-ybooks.co.uk

The Barbara Cartland Eternal Collection

The Barbara Cartland Eternal Collection is the unique opportunity to collect all five hundred of the timeless beautiful romantic novels written by the world's most celebrated and enduring romantic author.

Named the Eternal Collection because Barbara's inspiring stories of pure love, just the same as love itself, the books will be published on the internet at the rate of four titles per month until all five hundred are available.

The Eternal Collection, classic pure romance available worldwide for all time .

THE LATE DAME BARBARA CARTLAND

Barbara Cartland, who sadly died in May 2000 at the grand age of ninety eight, remains one of the world's most famous romantic novelists. With worldwide sales of over one billion, her outstanding 723 books have been translated into thirty six different languages, to be enjoyed by readers of romance globally.

Writing her first book 'Jigsaw' at the age of 21, Barbara became an immediate bestseller. Building upon this initial success, she wrote continuously throughout her life, producing bestsellers for an astonishing 76 years. In addition to Barbara Cartland's legion of fans in the UK and across Europe, her books have always been immensely popular in the USA. In 1976 she achieved the unprecedented feat of having books at numbers 1 & 2 in the prestigious B. Dalton Bookseller bestsellers list.

Although she is often referred to as the 'Queen of Romance', Barbara Cartland also wrote several historical biographies, six autobiographies and numerous theatrical plays as well as books on life, love, health and cookery. Becoming one of Britain's most popular media personalities and dressed in her trademark pink, Barbara spoke on radio and television about social and political issues, as well as making many public appearances.

In 1991 she became a Dame of the Order of the British Empire for her contribution to literature and her work for humanitarian and charitable causes.

Known for her glamour, style, and vitality Barbara

Cartland became a legend in her own lifetime. Best remembered for her wonderful romantic novels and loved by millions of readers worldwide, her books remain treasured for their heroic heroes, plucky heroines and traditional values. But above all, it was Barbara Cartland's overriding belief in the positive power of love to help, heal and improve the quality of life for everyone that made her truly unique.

AUTHOR'S NOTE

The background to this story of the Symbolists and the Left Bank of Paris in 1893 is correct.

The descriptions of the *Soleil d'Or*, Paul Verlaine, Joseph Péladan and Léo Taxil are all accurate. The Marquis de Guaita held strange séances and undermined his health by keeping himself awake night after night with morphine and hashish. He practised astral projection and believed himself haunted by *larvae* (imperfect apparitions of souls). He became half crazed and died at the age of thirty-six.

La Goulue fell on hard times. She became a wrestler, a lion-tamer and a servant in a brothel before ending up half rag-picker, half beggar. She lived in a wretched caravan and the only relic of her success was a piece of lace from her exciting *Can-Can* petticoats. She made it into a curtain 'which was grey with dust'. She died in 1929.

CHAPTER ONE
1892

"Emmeline Nevada Holtz! You will do as I say!"

There was a little laugh and a girl's voice answered,

"Now I know, Mama, that you are annoyed with me, because you call me 'Emmeline' only when you are angry!"

"Very well then – Vada!" was the concession, "although I cannot imagine why your father should have permitted you to use such a ridiculous nickname!"

"My real names are ridiculous!" Vada replied. "But I had the good sense at the age of two or whatever I was when I first began to talk to shorten one to Vada."

"The names we chose for you are very American!"

"Of course, Mama. Who would want to be anything else?"

The girl speaking rose to her feet and walked across the elaborate, luxuriously furnished New York drawing room to look out onto Central Park.

The trees were just beginning to show green and the tulips were brilliant in the flowerbeds.

"I am happy here with you," Vada said after a moment. "I have no wish to go to England."

"But I want you to go, my dear, and what is more I am determined that you shall do as I say, in this instance if in nothing else!"

Vada turned from the window to look at her mother. Mrs. Holtz was sitting on a sofa by the fire and her legs were covered with an ermine rug edged with sable.

A week ago, after their plans had been made to visit

England, she had wrenched her back severely whilst descending from her carriage and the doctor had said it was essential that she should remain immobile for at least two months.

Very attractive with fair hair that was just fading into grey, Mrs. Holtz had been a 'Southern Belle' when her husband had married her.

But her beauty had never equalled that of their only child. Emmeline, or rather 'Vada', as she preferred to be called in the home circle, was stunningly beautiful.

Her mother watched her with an appreciative eye as she crossed the room, her feet making no sound on the thick carpet.

Reaching the sofa, she knelt down beside her mother.

Her hair, so fair that it was the colour of spring corn not yet ripened by the sun, was swept back from a perfect oval forehead below which were two very large dark blue eyes, naturally fringed with dark lashes.

They were, Mrs. Holtz had always averred, inherited from some not too distant Irish ancestor who had crossed the Atlantic to seek freedom and perhaps a fortune in the New World.

Vada's eyes certainly seemed to dominate her face, but she had beneath a perfectly curved mouth a strong, determined little chin, which gave her face the character that was lacking in many beautiful women.

"Let me stay with you, Mama!" she pleaded.

But, if Vada was determined, her mother was more so. It was Mrs. Holtz who had always been the driving force in the family.

Her husband might have been one of the richest oil-kings in America who ruled his considerable Empire with an iron hand, but at home he was very much under the thumb of his lovely self-willed wife.

"No, Vada," Mrs. Holtz said now. "I have made my plans and I do not intend for them to be interrupted by anything so infuriating as a strained back."

"We can go when you are better, Mama. After all, how could I manage in England without you?"

"Perhaps it is all meant," Mrs. Holtz said philosophically. "I often feel that you might be more assertive when I am not there. Pretty mothers often tend to eclipse their daughters!"

Vada laughed.

"But I like being eclipsed, Mama! Besides, what would I have to say to the Duke without you putting the right words into my mouth?"

"That is just the whole point, Vada," her mother said sharply. "You have to stand on your own feet. It is you who are going to marry the Duke. Not me!"

Vada rose from her knees to sit down on a stool facing the fire.

The flames glinted with gold lights on her fair hair and her face was very serious as she said quietly, so quietly that her mother had difficulty in hearing,

"I cannot do it, Mama! I am sorry, but I cannot marry anyone I don't love!"

Mrs. Holtz made an exclamation of annoyance.

"Now really, Vada, it is far too late for you to be thinking of such nonsense! As I told you before, there is no one in America whom you can marry, but no one!"

There was a hint of mischief in Vada's eyes that swept away her serious expression.

"We are a very large country, Mama, and there are an

awful lot of men in it."

"You know exactly what I mean," Mrs. Holtz said sharply. "In the Social world in which we live I can think of no young man at this particular moment who is your equal financially."

"That is the real answer, Mama," Vada said. "There are plenty of young men, as you well know, who honour the *debutantes'* balls with their presence and who would be prepared to offer for me."

"Do you think for one moment that if you accepted one of those callow youths you are speaking about," Mrs. Holtz asked, "you would ever believe that they were more interested in you than in your millions?"

Vada was silent and her mother went on in a quieter voice,

"I have explained to you before, Vada, that it is impossible, quite impossible, ever to separate a person from his or her possessions. How can a man for instance say, 'would you love me if I was not the President, not the Prince of Wales and not Caruso?'"

She paused.

"You will admit it is impossible to think of them without the frame in which you see them, without the trappings with which they are embellished! And it is the same for you."

"Are you saying," Vada asked, "that no man will ever love me for myself?"

"Of course not!" Mrs. Holtz replied. "You will, I hope, be loved by many people in your life, but, when it comes to marriage, how can you be confident after a few meetings with a man at balls or receptions that he loves you for yourself alone?"

"You mean that he sees me through a golden haze?" Vada asked.

"Exactly!" her mother agreed. "It's a very good simile. You are haloed, encircled, framed with the glamour of being a millionairess – the richest girl in America!"

There was silence and then Mrs. Holtz said coaxingly,

"I love you, Vada, and that is why I am trying to do what is best for you now and for the future."

"By marrying me to a man I have never seen and whose only interest in me we know to be my riches?" Vada asked and her voice was sarcastic.

"Exactly!" Mrs. Holtz said positively. "And that is why I have chosen a man who has something to give in return! What have American men got that is better than or even equal to what you can offer them?"

Vada was silent and after a moment her mother went on,

"But an English Duke can offer you a position that is superior to any other in the world with the exception of Royalty."

"I am only surprised," Vada said, "that you don't aspire to a Prince!"

"I certainly would if there was one available!" Mrs. Holtz retorted. "But real Royalty, if they are worthy of the name, marry someone who is Royal. Others who call themselves Princes, like the Italians, are usually extremely bogus."

"I know you have studied the subject very carefully, Mama," Vada said in a voice that made it sound far from a compliment.

"I have studied it," Mrs. Holtz replied, "because I want for my only child the best that the world can give.

Although you don't think so, I want nothing but your happiness."

Vada rose from the stool to stand at the end of the sofa.

"What you are forgetting in all this, Mama," she said, "are my own feelings. I have a heart and, whilst like other girls of my age I want to be married, I also want to fall in love!"

Mrs. Holtz sighed.

"It is only the very young," she said, "who are so insatiably greedy that they forget to be grateful."

"What do you mean by that?" Vada enquired.

"I mean," her mother answered, "that you ask too much of life. Nothing is perfect. No one's existence is without some penalties and some discomforts attached to it."

She paused to note that her daughter was listening intently.

"You have so much you should be grateful for," she went on. "A happy home, many comforts, great beauty, a huge fortune, and yet you want more! You want the love of an outsider. A man you have not yet seen and a Fairytale romance such as only exists in novelettes."

"But that is natural!" Vada asserted. "It must be natural!"

"What will be natural," her mother said, "will be for you to fall in love with your husband and he with you after you are married. That is what happens in millions of marriages all over the world."

Vada was silent and Mrs. Holtz continued,

"Marriages are always arranged in France and I understand that they are extremely successful. Marriages have been arranged in England since the Norman Conquest usually because a bride could bring her husband a dowry of land that fitted in with his."

"Or money to buy more," Vada murmured beneath her breath.

"In the East," Mrs. Holtz continued, warming to her theme, "the bride and bridegroom never meet until the actual Wedding Ceremony. Everything is arranged by the matchmakers, astrologers and soothsayers and yet in India there is no question of divorce."

"Let's go back to England!" Vada said. "You cannot pretend that there are not many scandals among the aristocracy, because I have read about them."

"Then you had no right to do so." Mrs. Holtz said sharply. "I have always tried to keep the vulgar and sensational newspapers from you."

"But there are scandals, are there not?" Vada enquired.

"If there are scandals, they occur after marriage." Mrs. Holtz replied. "I am not pretending that there is not a great deal of gossip about the Prince of Wales and his associations with certain beautiful ladies."

She paused and added,

"But he always behaves in a most circumspect manner towards his wife, Princess Alexandra, and officially they are very happy."

"Is that the sort of marriage you are suggesting for me?" Vada asked.

"I am suggesting nothing of the sort." her mother replied coldly. "If you are clever with your husband, Vada, as I was with your father, it is very unlikely that he will look at another woman."

"And if he does?" Vada insisted.

Mrs. Holtz spread out her white hands, which glittered with several diamond rings.

"Would you be very much worse off with an English Duke, who strayed from your side, than an American who could leave you nothing but unhappy memories?"

"You mean being a Duchess and having a coronet on my head should compensate for everything?"

"It will compensate for a great deal," Mrs. Holtz answered. "At least you will start your marriage knowing that you will not feel every time your husband is nice to you that he is wondering how soon he can ask you to write a cheque for which you will obtain nothing in return."

"It's all so sordid! So horrible!" Vada exclaimed almost violently.

"Dearest, do believe that what I am doing is the best for you. There is no happiness here for you in America. Of that I am sure."

"I like America – I *love* America! It's my country!" Vada declared.

"And there are no women in the world who transplant better than American women," Mrs. Holtz answered. "They have an adaptability, Vada, that no other country has managed to achieve."

"I don't wish to be adaptable!" Vada murmured sulkily.

Mrs. Holtz did not speak and after a moment her daughter went on,

"I don't believe that Papa would have wanted me to marry someone from abroad, least of all an English Nobleman!"

"That is where you are wrong!" Mrs. Holtz replied.

"Your father agreed with me, as he always did, that when you were old enough we would have to choose your husband for you."

Vada made an impatient gesture but she did not interrupt and her mother continued,

"Your father knew from the very moment you were born that you were different from other children. That was why you were brought up as you were, quietly in the country, away from newspaper reporters and all the vulgarity and publicity that surrounds the children of other rich men."

"Papa was afraid of my being kidnapped!"

"Of course," Mrs. Holtz agreed. "Need I say that is why you have never been photographed, Vada? And you have never had your portrait painted."

She looked at her daughter for a moment and added a little wistfully,

"I would have loved to have a big portrait of you looking as you do now or even a sketch by that clever young man whose drawings I admire. What's his name?"

"Charles Dana Gibson," Vada replied automatically.

"Yes, Gibson," Mrs. Holtz repeated, "and I really believe that he could do you justice. You are in fact almost a perfect 'Gibson girl', as they call his models."

She sighed and went on,

"But your father would never countenance pictures of you appearing in the social journals and certainly not in those sordid 'rags' that are sold on street corners."

"I believe he fixed the editors of most of the newspapers," Vada said.

"Of course he did! Your father could do anything and besides he owned a number of newspapers himself.

Anyway lack of publicity is one of the reasons that you have been able to lead a quiet life and why I am determined that you shall not be submitted to the vulgarity that usually attends American *debutantes*."

"I have no wish to go to New York balls or mix with people who don't want me," Vada said almost defiantly.

"They want you all right," Mrs. Holtz retorted, "but nothing in New York is as impressive, spectacular or has such quality as the functions you will attend in England."

"As a – Duchess?"

"As a Duchess."

Vada was silent for a moment and then she said,

"I have a proposition to make to you, Mama. Let me live an ordinary social life, meeting anyone you choose in New York or any other part of America for just one year. After that, if I meet no one I like and no one I could – love, I will go to England."

Mrs. Holtz laughed.

"Really, Vada. How can you be so naïve? So incredibly foolish as to believe that English Dukes are waiting about until it suits some American heiress to pick them as if they were mushrooms?"

She laughed again.

"No, my dear, it is not at all easy to find a Duke. There are only about thirty of them and they have a very good idea of their own consequence!"

Vada gazed at her mother and Mrs. Holtz went on,

"If I had not been at school in Florence with the Duke's mother, you would never have had this opportunity, but our friendship has continued all through the years."

She paused.

"When the Dowager Duchess came to America six years ago, she stayed with us on Long Island. It was then that we talked together, a little guardedly, but nevertheless with perfect understanding of what might happen when you were old enough."

"I remember the Duchess," Vada said. "She was rather awe-inspiring."

"She comes from a very old English family," Mrs. Holtz explained, "and, as her father's lands, he was a Marquis, marched with those of the Duke of Grantham, it was obviously sensible that the two families should be united in marriage."

"Then she must have known the Duke since she was young." Vada said. "It is quite different travelling to England to marry someone one has never seen."

"You will meet each other and you will become engaged," Mrs. Holtz persisted. "There is no question of a hurried marriage or anything like that."

She gave a little sigh of satisfaction.

"And I promise you, Vada, it will be the most spectacular, the most sensational Wedding America has ever seen."

"You really think I would like that?" Vada asked.

"All sensible girls enjoy their Weddings," Mrs. Holtz snapped. "It's the one time in your life when you have no rivals and no equals. You are the bride and the focus of everyone's attention."

"Then, when the Wedding is over, you are left alone with your bridegroom," Vada said in a somewhat forlorn voice.

"In your case a bridegroom you can respect, a man you meet on equal terms. If you bring him a large fortune, he brings you a position and title, which none can equal."

There was silence in the room and then Vada rose to walk restlessly across to the piano.

She struck a note, sat down and played the opening bars of Mendelssohn's *Wedding March*. Then, closing the piano lid, she rose from the stool to walk across to the window.

"There is no alternative," Mrs. Holtz said quietly. "I promise you, Vada, you will be far happier my way than leaving anything to that deceptive, perfidious and often cruel emotion called love."

Vada did not turn from the window and after a moment Mrs. Holtz went on in a brisk voice,

"Everything is arranged and Miss Nancy Sparling has promised to chaperone you, until she actually hands you over to the Duke's mother."

"Nancy Sparling?" Vada asked.

"Yes, dear. You remember her? She is the Bishop of New York's sister and a very charming woman. She travels a great deal and I shall not worry in the slightest if you are in her care."

"When are we leaving?" Vada asked in a low voice.

There was a light of triumph in Mrs. Holtz's eyes, as she realised that her daughter had accepted the inevitable.

"Next week."

"Next week?" Vada repeated, turning from the window. "But that is impossible!"

"Why?" her mother enquired.

"Surely I shall have to buy new clothes for one thing?"

"I have thought of that," Mrs. Holtz said. "I don't want the newspapers to learn that you are going to Europe, in which case they might so easily have a suspicion that there is an ulterior motive in your journey. So you will buy all the clothes you will need in Paris."

"I am going to Paris?" Vada asked and now there was an interest in her voice that had not been there before.

"That is what I have planned," Mrs. Holtz said, "and bitterly disappointed I am that I cannot come with you. Paris in the spring is every American woman's idea of Heaven!"

There was a reminiscent smile on her lips before she went on,

"Fortunately Nancy Sparling knows Paris as well as I do, if not better. She actually lived there for some months and she will therefore, Vada, take you to all the right *couturiers*. Worth, Doucet, Rouff."

"That at least sounds interesting."

"I want you to be very smart and very appropriately dressed when you reach England," Mrs. Holtz continued. "Nowhere in the world can you find such entrancing clothes as in Paris. That, if nothing else, Vada, should make you look forward to the trip."

"I will look forward to seeing Paris," Vada said. "It's a place I have always longed to visit. You know, Mama, how interested I have been in the new art and in the new thought that always seems to come from the French Capital?"

"I certainly don't want you to waste your time on that sort of nonsense!" Mrs. Holtz said sharply. "The English are very conventional and as for art, they have fabulous pictures in every aristocratic home that cannot be equalled by any other country in the world."

Vada said nothing.

There was a light in her eyes that had not been there

before.

"Anyway, a week in Paris should give you plenty of time to buy everything you require," Mrs. Holtz went on. "Some of the gowns may have to be sent on, but the French are so clever that they can provide a whole trousseau in half the time that any other dressmaker requires for one simple gown."

"I want to see Paris in the spring!" Vada said quietly as if to herself.

"That is exactly what you will see," Mrs. Holtz answered, "and, Vada, you will behave with great propriety, remembering that your visit to Paris is only a prelude to your appearance in England."

She paused to add impressively,

"I would want you to be not only the most beautiful American Duchess but the most circumspect."

"I will try, Mama. But there is one thing I want to say."

"What is that?" Mrs. Holtz asked.

"It is this," Vada answered. "If the Duke and I really dislike each other, if we feel that there can be no possible bond between us, then whatever anyone may say I shall refuse to marry him."

"It is such an unlikely contingency," Mrs. Holtz said loftily, "that I have no intention of discussing it with you. The Duke is a charming, cultured, exceedingly well bred Englishman. If you meet him in the spirit in which I am quite certain he is prepared to meet you, you will undoubtedly find an affinity together."

"I hope so, Mama," Vada said in a low voice.

She was about to say more, but a maid entered the room and approached the sofa.

"The masseuse is here, Mrs. Holtz."

"Oh, thank you, Jessie," Mrs. Holtz answered. "Ask Carlos to bring in the wheelchair to take me to the bedroom."

"I'll do that, Mrs. Holtz," the maid answered and she went from the room.

"I am not sending Jessie with you to Europe," Mrs. Holtz said to Vada as the door closed. "She would not fit in at all well with English servants."

"What you mean, Mama, is she is too familiar calling you 'Mrs. Holtz' instead of 'madam'," Vada said with a smile. "That is American independence!"

"Something they don't appreciate in the Old Country," Mrs. Holtz remarked. "You will therefore take Charity with you."

"Oh, good!" Vada exclaimed. "I would rather travel with Charity than anyone else, even though, as you well know, Mama, she is very inclined to nanny me."

"She will look after you. That is all that matters," Mrs. Holtz said. "Charity is the old-fashioned type of servant who knows her place, but at the same time can be relied upon. She has travelled a great deal with me and I will miss her when you are gone. But Charity knows how to behave."

"She certainly will not gossip with the other servants as Jessie would," Vada said. "I would never be surprised, Mama, if Jessie did not sell her life story to one of the more sensational newspapers. Can you imagine how it would read – *My Years in the Oil-King's Palaces* or *'The Secrets of Loftus Holtz's Family and their Inhibitions'*?"

"Really, Vada," Mrs. Holtz exclaimed, "that is not funny."

"Only because I feel it is very near the truth," Vada

smiled.

"Your father had a horror of journalists and so have I," Mrs. Holtz said. "You must be very careful not to let anyone know that you are travelling to Europe or on which ship you are sailing. Your cabins, of course, will be booked simply in the name of Miss Nancy Sparling. No one will have any idea that she is accompanied by the wealthy Emmeline Holtz."

Vada laughed before she said,

"You know, Mama, we have for so many years been afraid of our own shadows and shied away from any possible mention of our name, that now I don't believe that the words 'Emmeline Holtz' would mean anything at all to the great American public!"

"It would mean a great deal once the newspaper boys got working on it," Mrs. Holtz said gravely, "and after that, Vada, you would never be able to appear anywhere without drawing a crowd, say anything without it being printed the next morning, buy a new hat or a new pair of shoes without someone speculating that you were going to do something sensational in them!"

Vada sighed.

"You are right, Mama. I would hate that."

"Then believe that the life your poor Papa mapped out for you was the right one and I am only carrying out his wishes."

As if the words moved her, Vada knelt down beside the sofa on which her mother sat and bent forward to kiss her.

"I love you, Mama! And so I am going to do what you wish and I will travel to Europe to have a look at the Duke."

"You will marry him, Vada!" Mrs. Holtz said quietly.

"I will think about it." Vada promised.

Mrs. Holtz rested her hand with a sudden gesture of affection against her daughter's cheek.

"You are very lovely, child. It would give me great joy to think of you at the Opening of Parliament, attending a State Ball at Buckingham Palace and curtseying to Queen Victoria wearing three white Prince of Wales's feathers in your hair."

"It all sounds very formal," Vada said, "and, when I drive away from Buckingham Palace in the three white feathers beside my husband glittering with his decorations, what do I talk to him about?"

"Now, Vada," Mrs. Holtz reproved, "those sort of questions only make things difficult for yourself."

"But those are the sort of questions that have to be answered sometime, Mama, have they not?"

"You will find a thousand things to interest you in England," Mrs. Holtz said enthusiastically, "and a thousand different subjects for conversation."

"Which will all be very appropriate except for one." Vada said.

"And what is that?" Mrs. Holtz enquired.

"Love!" Vada replied, "And that, you must admit, Mama, will not come easily to the tongue."

There was a silence and Mrs. Holtz touched her daughter's cheek again.

"You are being nonsensical, dearest," she said. "Promise me to go to England. That is all I will ask of you at the moment. Everything else will fall into place like a jigsaw puzzle when you get there. Now go and sort out the things you want to take with you. Not too many!

Remember, there is all that deliciously exciting shopping to be done in Paris."

"I have not forgotten – Paris," Vada affirmed.

She lowered her voice on the last word because the door opened and Jessie came in accompanied by a manservant pushing a wheelchair.

They lifted Mrs. Holtz very carefully from the sofa into the chair and the manservant pushed her across the room and along the wide corridor that led to her bedroom, which was situated on the same floor.

It was a very large ugly brown stone house and quite one of the most impressive in New York.

Vada had always thought it too large for her mother and her requirements after her father's death.

He had died two years ago and, after a year's mourning which they had spent on his various estates scattered all over America, they had come to New York for only two or three months to buy new clothes and to introduce Vada to some of her mother's friends.

She had been surprised at the time how very few parties she was permitted to attend and no balls.

There had been balls and parties for the younger people in the country ever since she could remember, but even when she was fifteen she had noticed how strictly chaperoned she was and how the liberties permitted to other girls of her age were barred where she was concerned.

When she danced with a young man, she was always returned immediately to her mother's side.

There was no question of her going on picnics or even to drive with her girlfriends without there being a chaperone with them. In Vada's case it was nearly always her mother.

Her friends were invited to her home, but even there she was seldom left alone with them for any length of time.

She had the feeling that girlish confidences were frowned upon.

It did not worry her particularly because there were so many ways in which she could occupy her time.

She loved reading for one thing and never a day would pass that she did not go riding, accompanied, of course, by a groom and often an older companion chosen by her mother.

The fact that she was on horseback and on one of the finest breeds was a delight in itself.

Vada could play the piano extremely well and the best teachers had always been employed by her father to develop this particular talent.

It somehow struck her as strange that even though her music teacher was an old man, her Governess, or in many instances Charity, always sat in the room during her lessons.

Vada sometimes felt that it must be boring for them, but at the same time she taught herself to concentrate completely on anything that she was doing and after a time she forgot their presence.

The same applied to her French and German lessons and the Italian operas she studied under an Italian teacher.

Her other teachers included Professors in the Classics and one who had a degree in English Literature.

When these were present, Vada's Governess, a delightful woman who had taught her her first lessons, was always present.

Miss Miribelle Channing was a woman whose

intelligence and intellect were unusual in an age when women were not supposed to be erudite in any way.

She taught Vada all she knew herself and then persuaded her father to augment her education with visiting Professors and more qualified teachers.

"You should have been a boy," Miss Channing said to Vada once. "You would have been a considerable help to your father."

"Why can I not help him now?" Vada asked.

"Because, dear, women are meant to sit at home and be nice, complacent wives and mothers," Miss Channing had replied.

"Supposing they don't get a husband?" Vada had asked, thinking of her Governess.

"In which case they can only wish that they had been born a man!" Miss Channing answered.

Vada had often thought of her words and yet, she told herself, she had no wish to be a man.

She wanted to be a woman. But she wanted a far wider and more interesting life than the average woman enjoyed.

It was true that there was talk of feminine emancipation and the young American girls, she had learnt, were allowed far more licence than their mothers had enjoyed.

Even so, it seemed to Vada that they were very restricted, so much so that the subjects they were interested in and on which they could speak seemed incredibly limited.

She realised that she was different from the large majority of her contemporaries in that her education had been so extensive.

Once she had said to Miss Channing,

"I know I have you to thank for all I have been taught and for all I have been able to learn. Without you I should merely have been painting watercolours or sewing samplers."

"Knowledge is a great compensation for the lack of other things," Miss Channing told her.

Vada had felt that there was a kind of meaning in her voice, as if she was giving her a message.

Now, as her mother left the room, Vada sat down on the floor in front of the fire and quite inadvertently Miss Channing's words came back to her.

"*Knowledge is a great compensation for the lack of other things* – "

'Will knowledge be a compensation for love?' she asked herself.

Would knowledge make her feel less envious of women who were loved solely because they were women, not because they were encompassed with money?

She had never really considered her wealth before.

But now when she thought of the millions that her father had left her on his death and the millions of dollars accumulating year after year as more and more oil gushed from the wells he owned, she realised that her mother was right when she said that she was not like other girls.

How could any man consider her separately from that golden pedestal on which she was perched high above all ordinary mortals?

The whole of America was obsessed with the desire for gold. They slaved for it, they worked for it, they imagined it, they dreamt of it.

More and more money! Gold that could buy, they believed, everything a man or woman could desire.

'Except for one thing,' Vada told herself, ' – love!'

A coal dropped in the grate and she rose to her feet, remembering that her mother would expect her to change her dress in time for tea.

It was one of the ways, Vada told herself, that the rich occupied their leisure hours, by the endless changing of clothes.

There were morning gowns in which they breakfasted, street clothes in which they went driving, special gowns for luncheon parties and afternoon gowns in which they would attend *soirées* or receptions.

At teatime every American lady changed again into a special gown that was soft and feminine and which seemed somehow in accord with the silver teapot on a silver tray slavishly copied from what was used in England by their social counterparts.

Then, of course, for dinner, even for a family dinner party, there was the décolleté evening gown in which they descended the stairs to dazzle the eyes of perhaps no more than one or two indifferent servants.

'Change – change – change!' Vada said to herself as she went along the corridor. 'I am sure it's part of some gigantic pattern, perhaps a game played by someone who manipulates us poor humans as if we were pawns.'

She laughed at her own imagination, but, when she reached her own room, she stood gazing at it with a sudden feeling of dissatisfaction.

It was so artificially decorated, a conception of what a young girl should have as an idealised bedroom.

There were white flounces round the brass bedstead with its ornate back and foot. The petticoated, white muslin dressing table was threaded through with little pink

~22~

ribbons tied in bows.

The curtains, also pink, were befringed, tasselled and tied back with frilled lace and velvet ropes that gave the impression of frivolous children.

The furniture was all hand-painted with birds and flowers and was festooned with small *objets d'art* of every sort.

Vada could not remember a birthday or a Christmas when her mother had not, among a profusion of other gifts, given her pieces of china. Some were Dresden shepherdesses. Others were porcelain and silver and gold or semi-precious stones.

Most of them were of people and animals, although some were just amusing little boxes of no great value, but definitely of the type that should be to the taste of a young girl.

The whole constituted a clutter in her bedroom that she had often longed to sweep away.

But her mother would have been horrified at the idea, just as she would not have understood that Vada was tired of the pictures that decorated the walls.

Pictures of children playing with animals, reproductions of Sir Joshua Reynolds's *Age of Innocence* or pictures by other notable artists, who idealised animals.

There were also a number of sacred subjects, too gaudy and fanciful to have any touch of reality about them.

'It's not only a child's room, but the room of a halfwit,' Vada told herself and then was ashamed of being so critical.

Her mother had said that she was ungrateful and she tried to tell herself how lucky she was to have such a room all to herself.

There were homeless people, as she well knew, walking the streets of New York, with families huddled together in garrets or basements where there was hardly room to turn round.

But she could only feel that her bedroom, like her private sitting room, was an insult to her intelligence.

It was the same in every house they owned.

The rooms were almost identical except for colouring and, when they travelled, Vada's special possessions travelled with them.

The china, the *objets d'art* and the little boxes were all brought along as part of the luggage.

Similarly, when she had been small, her dolls, her Teddy bear, her Fairy story books were all carried from place to place so that she should feel at home.

The result of it all was that Vada felt constrained by chains that bound her as if they encircled her wrists and her ankles.

There was no escape from the familiar. It was the same, she sometimes thought, with her mind.

It was impossible for her to think for herself and to make any sort of decision.

Sometimes she would try just to see if she could change the existing order.

"Instead of riding tomorrow morning," she would say, "I should like to ride in the afternoon."

"But Professor Haber is coming to you after luncheon, Vada. Had you forgotten?"

"Why can he not come after breakfast instead?"

"And what would be the point of that?" her mother or Miss Channing would ask.

There was no answer to such a question and the

curriculum continued as it had before and it seemed to Vada at times as though nothing could ever change.

There were even houses and estates they always visited at special times in the year.

There was one for the spring, one for the autumn, one for the heat of the summer, and one for the cold winter months.

It was like walking about on a chessboard, Vada thought, on which every square was exactly the same except for its colour.

She used to imagine herself moving from the yellow square that was spring to the pink square that was summer onto the brown square that was autumn and the white square that was winter.

Then on again in exactly the same rotation to a square of exactly the same size, all of them leading nowhere.

'It is selfish of me to complain. It is wrong to be so discontented. I am so lucky! I am so fortunate! I am so rich!' Vada told herself.

It was all like a gigantic house of cards and one thing she would like to do would be to knock it all down.

But now for the first time in her life she was about to do something different!

She felt her spirits rise.

At least she would see Paris, even if only for one week. At least the monotony and the familiarity of America would be left behind.

It was frightening to think of what might happen when she reached England, but she would not let herself dwell on that.

Instead she would remember that she would see so much she had read about, so much she had longed to discover, to understand and to touch.

Paris in the spring!

For the first time Vada felt as if the golden cage in which she had been incarcerated ever since she had been born had an open window.

Only a small window, but nevertheless it was open!

Chapter Two

"We reach France tomorrow," Miss Nancy Sparling declared.

"I know," Vada answered, "it's so exciting I can hardly believe it!"

Miss Sparling smiled.

She was a large heavily-built woman with a face not unlike a good-looking horse.

Related on her mother's side to most of the important families in America and daughter of the Bishop of New York, she moved in the very best Society, not only in America but in most European countries.

Vada had learnt that it was by way of being a great condescension for her to consent to act the part of chaperone.

Nancy Sparling had been independent ever since she had been a girl.

Realising early in life that she was not attractive to the opposite sex, she had taken up an independent attitude, which, surprisingly, had been encouraged by her parents.

By the time she was thirty she had travelled almost all over the world and at the age of fifty she had a personality that had made her popular with the great American public.

Dressed always in the latest fashion when she appeared at the first night of a new play, the opening of the opera or dined at the White House, there was not a newspaper that did not describe her appearance.

If possible they also printed her comments for their Society-conscious readers to devour avidly the following day.

When the three women embarked on the British liner that was to carry them to Europe, it was Nancy Sparling who gave interviews to the press, cracked a joke with the reporters she knew and who swept on board like a Prima Donna.

Vada crept onto the ship by another gangplank escorted only by Charity to gain the sanctuary of their cabins where she remained until they sailed.

"Your mother should be pleased with me," Miss Sparling said when she joined Vada. "There was not a reporter there who had the slightest idea that I was not travelling alone."

She gave a little laugh.

"How angry they would be if they knew what a scoop they have missed!"

"Don't talk about it," Vada begged her. "I don't want anyone to suspect the reason I am going to England."

"I don't blame you!" Miss Sparling said sharply. "Nothing is more deflating to a romance than to have it mouthed over and publicised before it takes place."

"Perhaps it will never take place," Vada commented quietly.

"You had better not let your mother hear you say that," Miss Sparling answered. "She has set her heart on your being a Duchess."

"I know," Vada answered. "At the same time – "

Miss Sparling glanced at the expression on Vada's face and said briskly,

"Now don't let's depress ourselves by anticipating what lies ahead. Our first stop is Paris and that is something for you to be really excited about."

"It is indeed!" Vada agreed.

They talked of Paris for most of the voyage and Vada was fascinated by hearing of the people Nancy Sparling had met on previous visits.

"Is it really as gay and naughty as everyone says?" Vada asked.

Nancy Sparling laughed.

"The last time I went to Paris I was accompanied by my father, because he longed to see *Notre Dame* before he died. He said that it was the greatest and most spiritual experience he had ever had."

"I see what you mean," Vada said. "Paris means different things to different people."

"As do all places in the world. But you have one great advantage, Emmeline, over most other travellers, especially American girls."

"What is that?" Vada asked with interest.

"You are not only intelligent," Nancy Sparling replied. "You are also very well read."

She saw the surprise on Vada's face and went on,

"You have no idea how shallowly most girls are educated. It's bad enough in America where men worship women, but want them to be complacent housewives and little else, while in England – "

She paused.

"What about England?" Vada asked.

"English girls are lucky if they have lessons with a Governess who has read anything except the Bible and *The Ladies' Journal.*"

As Vada looked at her with curiosity, Nancy Sparling went on,

"All the money in an English family is spent on educating the men. The sons come first in everything. The few crumbs that are left from what they require, and they are very few, are spent on a young man's miserable sisters."

"You make me sorry for them." Vada said.

"You can be." Nancy Sparling answered, "and I assure you that they are worthy of your compassion. At the same time, astonishingly, a large number of English women turn out to be quick-witted, fascinating and very alluring."

"I see I shall have quite a lot of competition," Vada smiled.

"Not when it comes to your looks and your money," Nancy Sparling replied.

She saw Vada wince and added,

"Face up to facts, Emmeline, there is no point in your shying like a nervous foal every time anyone mentions money. You can be rich and proud of it. Why not?"

"I hate my money!" Vada exclaimed.

"That is the only stupid remark I have ever heard you make," Nancy Sparling replied. "Money can always be utilised for good in one way or another. But if it overshadows your life and if it affects the development of your character, then it automatically becomes evil."

"What can I do about it?" Vada asked and there was a little throb in her voice that the elder woman did not miss.

"Stick that determined little chin of yours in the air," she answered, "and be proud of it, as you are proud of being American. Be strong! Be determined! We women can go a good long way to conquering the world if we make up our minds to do it."

Vada sighed.

"You are brave. I am afraid of what the future will hold."

"So was I when I was your age and I did not have half

your advantages, but I made up my mind I would get what I wanted and with a few exceptions I have done just that."

"And what did you want?" Vada asked.

Nancy Sparling thought for a moment.

"If I say 'to see the world', it sounds banal," she answered. "There was that and so much more. I wanted to find out about life. I wanted to live fully and that is exactly what I have done."

"I envy you," Vada said in all sincerity.

"If you say that to me in five years' time, I will believe you," Nancy Sparling answered. "At the moment you are just hatching out of the egg, a comfortable, enveloping cotton wool egg in which you have been protected ever since you were born. The world outside is sometimes cold and treacherous, but it is also adventurous and very exciting."

It was exciting, Vada told herself, the following day as the liner accompanied by hooting tugs moved slowly into the harbour at Cherbourg.

Vada, standing on deck, saw the beautiful natural bay protected on every side except from the North.

She could see the huge breakwater begun by Louis XIV and completed by Louis XVI and Napoleon Bonaparte.

'I am stepping into a history book,' she told herself ecstatically.

Their passage from New York had been somewhat rough, which had kept a large number of the passengers in their cabins.

There was not, Nancy Sparling pointed out, anyone particularly interesting on board.

Most of the travellers were rich Americans,

businessmen who stayed in the smoking room, talking a language all of their own until the early hours of the morning, and a few aspiring Socialites who tried to approach Vada only to be snubbed quite unmercifully by Nancy Sparling.

"I just cannot be bothered with those sorts of people." she said to Vada, "nor need you be. They are not really interested in us as persons, they only want to go back and tell their friends in Brooklyn what close friends we became on the voyage to Europe."

Nancy Sparling, as she spoke, mimicked the ingratiating tones of the people who had aspired to their acquaintance and Vada found herself laughing helplessly.

She knew, as the voyage ended, that she had never had a more entertaining or amusing companion.

At home her mother monopolised the guests and the conversation and it was impossible for Vada to be assertive in her presence or indeed to contribute anything of interest to what was being said.

To have someone like Nancy Sparling asking her opinion and listening to what she had to say was a pleasure that she had never experienced before in her quiet cloistered life.

Nancy Sparling was very scathing about the way Vada had been brought up.

"Both your father and mother were fanatical on the subject of publicity," she said. "Most of it is just good healthy American curiosity. There is no harm in it. Of course the newspapers pull the leg of a celebrity from time to time and why not? A little criticism does nobody any harm."

"I wish you would tell Mama that," Vada said.

"Equally it's a relief not to be written about as I have noticed some girls have been."

"They would cry their eyes out if they were not constantly mentioned," Nancy Sparling added tartly.

Most of the time they talked about Paris, one subject being the Impressionists about whom Nancy Sparling knew a great deal.

Unlike most Americans, she had made an effort to understand what they were trying to depict.

"I have bought one or two of their paintings," she said, "and I shall acquire some more on this trip, although we will not have much time if we are to buy half the gowns for your trousseau that your mother expects."

"Oh, don't let's buy too many!" Vada begged. "I loathe fittings! It's so boring. I want to explore Paris. I want to see the *Champs Élysées*, the Eiffel Tower, *Notre Dame* and, of course the *cafés* and perhaps – "

She glanced at Nancy from under her eyelashes.

" – the *Moulin Rouge*!"

"Your mother would have a heart attack if she heard you!" Nancy Sparling answered.

She did not say whether or not she would take Vada to such a place.

Looking and listening to Nancy Sparling made Vada wonder whether a woman could not really be happy without a home and a husband.

It was something she had never really considered.

'Supposing,' she asked herself, 'I never marry? I could travel. I could have friends all over the world.'

Then she knew that it would not be enough for her. She wanted to be married, but most of all she wanted to love and be loved.

But how little she knew about it!

She had watched her father and mother when they were together, but somehow, although her father obviously had been very fond of his wife, it was difficult to think of them as wildly in love with each other. What was this emotion that authors wrote about, which inspired painters and because of which Kings like Ludwig I of Bavaria were forced to abdicate?

Vada was very innocent. Mrs. Holtz had seen to that!

Nakedness was considered disgusting. Passion was something of which a girl should know nothing. The mystery of childbirth was an undiscussible subject.

'I wish someone would tell me about love,' Vada thought as they neared France.

Paris was the City of Love – *L'amour* brought a gleam to old men's eyes when they spoke of Paris – why? What was the magic of this emotion that seemed to be centred in Paris?

The secret as far as a woman was concerned seemed to lie with a man.

But what man, what must he be like? Would the Duke bring her the wild overwhelming wonder that to some people was like the Holy Grail and to others something so low and debauched that Vada could not even imagine what it would be?

It was a mystery, something she could not understand, but which she yearned for.

Love – but for whom?

*

The train that would carry them to Paris was waiting

alongside the quay.

Their heavy leather trunks were stowed in the guard's van. Charity was fussing over a small bag that she thought had been left behind, while an official resplendent in gold braid escorted them to the compartment that had been reserved in the name of 'Miss Nancy Sparling'.

They climbed in and it was the right word, because as usual, although Vada did not know it before, French trains were much higher than the Station platform.

They had settled themselves against the comfortable cushioned seats when Nancy Sparling gave an exclamation.

"How stupid of me!" she said. "I left my gloves on the bookstall when we were looking at the magazines."

"I will get them for you," Vada suggested.

Her offer was too late.

Quickly because, despite her rather large build, Nancy Sparling moved as she talked, the elder woman opened the door of the carriage and stepped down onto the platform.

Either she had forgotten the train was higher than the trains in America or else she slipped.

Anyway, she fell and gave a shrill cry as she did so.

Vada started to her feet and, going to the door of the carriage, saw Nancy Sparling lying on the platform. Her handbag which had burst open as she fell had scattered its contents all around her.

"Are you – hurt?" Vada asked in dismay.

She jumped down beside Nancy Sparling and realised for the moment that she was almost incapable of speech.

"It's my leg," she said after a while. "I'm sure I have broken it!"

"Oh, no! You cannot have done!" Vada exclaimed.

Officials, porters and onlookers appeared as if by

magic.

Nancy Sparling in great pain was carried to the waiting room.

There was some delay while a doctor was sent for and it was obvious that it would be impossible for them to proceed in the train they had intended to travel on.

Their luggage was therefore taken out of the van and their belongings collected from the reserved carriage.

Charity and Vada sat beside Miss Sparling offering what consolation they could.

After fetching her a Cognac from the buffet, there was nothing else practical they could do until a doctor arrived.

When he did he looked serious.

"Madame will have to go to hospital," he said. "I don't know how bad her leg is, but obviously it must have immediate attention."

"I hate hospitals!" Nancy Sparling said in her fluent French. "Is not there a Convent, *monsieur*? They are always much more comfortable and the nuns are the best nurses in the world."

"*Oui, madame*, we have a Convent." the doctor replied, "and I am sure the nuns will look after you, as you say, better than we should be able to do in our not very adequate hospital."

"Very well, take me there," Nancy Sparling commanded.

It all took time.

When finally Nancy Sparling had been examined by the doctor and was in bed in a pleasant if sparsely furnished bedroom with a beautiful view over the harbour, Vada learnt with consternation that there would be no chance of their going to Paris as planned.

"It's not as bad as I first thought," the doctor had said. "Madame has a small fracture, which should heal in two or three weeks if she rests her leg completely."

"Two or three weeks?" Vada exclaimed.

While she was sorry for Nancy Sparling, she was also sorry for herself.

This meant that she would not see Paris.

She would have to stay in the small rather dull seaport until it was time to go to England.

Nancy Sparling, however, had very different ideas.

"Stay here with me?" she asked. "I have never heard anything so ridiculous!"

"What do you mean?" Vada asked in surprise.

"My dear child, you must go to Paris. You must have clothes. Your mother would never forgive me if you arrived in England without all the magnificent gowns from Worth and Doucet that she has envisaged you wearing. Besides, why should you miss the joy of seeing Paris through my stupidity?"

"But how can I go alone?" Vada asked.

"You will have Charity with you. A suite is engaged at the *Hotel Meurice* and surely you are not so faint-hearted that you cannot look after yourself for a few days?"

"I-I never thought of – such a thing," Vada stammered.

"It's about time you grew up!" Nancy Sparling remarked. "When I was eighteen, I had been all over the Americas including the Argentine and Mexico and I was planning a trip to Australia!"

"I don't like – to leave you," Vada said.

"I can assure you that I shall be quite safe here," Nancy Sparling said with laughter in her voice, "and you will be safe in Paris. Charity has been there often enough with your mother. She knows all the *couturiers* I was to take you to."

She paused to add,

"The only thing is I don't think it very wise to send you with a lot of introductions."

Vada did not speak and she went on,

"The French are conventional like the English. They would certainly expect you to be chaperoned. Actually I had not intended to look up many people while we were in Paris."

She sighed.

"Most of my friends are getting old just as I am and I thought that they would bore you! With all the clothes we have to buy in the short time we have, I felt that we should have quite enough to do on our own."

She smiled before she continued,

"We don't want to get involved in dinner parties and luncheons and those endless afternoon receptions where you sit about in gilt chairs and make polite conversation with people you have never seen before and hope to Heaven you will never see again!"

Vada laughed.

"I should hate to do that."

"I never intended you should," Nancy Sparling replied. "I really promised myself that we would be real tourists and just look at all the things you ought to see. You can do that quite well with Charity, so nobody will notice that I am not there with you."

"You mean I can go to *Notre Dame,* the Eiffel Tower and the *Bois de Boulogne* and perhaps sit in the *cafés* and watch the world go by?"

"Exactly! And, if you use your eyes and your imagination, you will not miss me in the slightest!"

"I shall do that." Vada said with a smile, "but I do want to go to Paris."

"Well then. Go!" Nancy Sparling said. "Personally I think it's a very good thing and your mother will not know about it until it's all over, so she will not worry."

She gave a little laugh.

"You cannot come to any harm at the *Hotel Meurice*, but just in case you feel a lack of confidence I will give you something I have always carried ever since I was your age. Give me that handbag."

She pointed to her expensive leather handbag that stood on the chest of drawers in a corner of the room and Vada took it to her.

Nancy Sparling opened it and drew out a small pistol.

It was so small that Vada thought for a moment it was only a toy.

"My father gave me this when I made my first trip," Nancy Sparling said. "He said to me then, 'I am quite convinced that you will never have any need to use this, but it's a very good deterrent, loaded or unloaded'."

She held it out to Vada.

"I have only fired it once," Nancy Sparling said, "except when I have been practising with it. Do you know how to use it?"

"Papa showed me how to shoot when we were on the ranch," Vada replied, "but I have never owned a pistol of my own."

"Now I will lend you mine. Put it in your handbag and forget about it, but if you do feel frightened at night, you can always keep it under your pillow."

"Yes, of course," Vada answered.

She took the pistol and the little box, which contained four bullets and put them into her handbag.

"Hurry!" Nancy Sparling ordered. "Find out when the next train leaves for Paris and mind you and Charity are on it!"

*

Vada could hardly believe it was true when finally she and Charity were once again in a reserved compartment and the wheels of the train were carrying them swiftly on their way.

"I don't know what your mother would say, Miss Vada," Charity grumbled, "I don't really! I never heard such a thing! Miss Sparling sending you off alone like this. It's not right! I'm sure it's not!"

"She knew that you could look after me adequately," Vada answered.

"Well, of course, I can," Charity replied in a more mollified tone.

"And you do see, Charity, that I have to have some clothes?" Vada continued. "We packed very few gowns simply because we knew that we should buy others in Paris."

"That's true," Charity agreed.

Looking at Charity sitting opposite her in the railway carriage, Vada thought that no one could have a more respectable-looking chaperone.

Dressed in black, which she always wore with just a touch of white at the neck, her grey hair drawn back severely from her square forehead, her plain untrimmed bonnet on top of her head, Charity looked the epitome of all that was austere and respectable in American family life.

She had been left on the steps of an orphanage when a baby and, with the unconscious cruelty of the age, they had christened her 'Charity' so that she would never forget that she had been taken in out of charity.

Loftus Holtz had contributed very generously to many orphanages and institutions and among them was the one that Charity had been brought up in.

Because she was a sensible hard-working girl, she had been introduced into his mother's household when she was quite young and, when he had married, she had become personal maid to the 'young Mrs. Holtz'.

Charity had adored Vada ever since she was born and Vada was well aware that she would not only look after her but would be a tower of defence in any trouble.

Determined to put her into a good temper, Vada said now,

"What fun we will have in Paris, Charity! You can show me all the places you went to with Mama. I don't want to miss anything."

"Your mother was never one for sight-seeing," Charity replied. "All she thought of was junketing about with all those high-titled French ladies, wearing her diamonds to the opera and going to restaurants that are very much smarter than anything we've got at home."

"I am afraid I shall not be able to do that," Vada said wistfully.

"You can't take me to them and that's a fact," Charity said. "Two women wouldn't be allowed in unaccompanied."

"Never mind," Vada said. "We can do all the other things. I long to climb to the top of the Eiffel Tower."

"It was not finished when I was last there," Charity said.

"I know," Vada replied. "It was specially designed for the Exhibition in 1889. It is 984 feet high and the guide books say it symbolises the creativity, vigour and brilliance of France's builders and engineers."

"That's as may be," Charity said tartly, "but buildings weren't meant to be as high as that."

Vada laughed, but she thought a little sadly how much she was going to miss Nancy Sparling.

Charity was always completely convinced that everything that was best was to be found in America and Vada was well aware that she would not have a very inspiring companion to explore Paris with.

But she was not complaining.

After all, it was so marvellous to think that she did not have to sit beside Nancy Sparling's bed, but could go off on her own.

At the same time she was a little afraid.

Supposing, because she was Emmeline Holtz, people forced themselves upon her?

She felt a little quiver of fear. She knew that her mother's determination to keep her away from the public eye had, despite all Nancy Sparling's disparaging remarks, had a great deal of sense in it.

She had seen the way other wealthy heiresses were pursued by the press. She had once been in the theatre when one of them had just announced her engagement.

All through the performance there had been reporters struggling to talk to her, photographers setting up their cameras and it had obviously been impossible for the girl to hear or enjoy one word of what was taking place on the stage.

'I should hate that!' she thought with a sudden shyness.

If Nancy Sparling had been with her, it would not have mattered, but to face it alone was something that made her shrink inside herself with something akin to terror.

She opened her handbag and took out some letters Nancy Sparling had given her and the tickets for the journey.

She read one from the *Hotel Meurice*, written to her mother in New York.

> *"We beg to advise you," it said in the most fulsome French, "that the suite you have engaged for your daughter, Miss Emmeline Holtz and her companion, Miss Nancy Sparling, is the very best and most luxurious in our hotel –"*

It went on to describe all the comforts that could be offered to those staying at the *Meurice and* Vada read it through carefully.

Then she said to Charity,

"I have an idea."

"What is it, Miss Vada?"

"Mama engaged the rooms for us at the hotel, but there is, of course, no description of either Miss Sparling or myself."

"Why should there be?" Charity asked in surprise.

"No reason at all," Vada said, "except that they will not know what we look like."

"You've only got to tell them who we are, Miss Vada."

"Yes, I know that." Vada said. "Nancy Sparling has

never been to the *Meurice*. It was Mama's choice. She told me that she always goes to the *Bristol* where the Prince of Wales stays."

"I'm sure the *Meurice* will make us very comfortable, Miss Vada," Charity said. "Last time we were in Paris, your mother and I were at the *Rivoli*, but we didn't like it and that's why Madam decided that you should go to the *Meurice*."

"So they will not know you either," Vada said in a quiet voice.

Charity looked at her in perplexity and Vada went on,

"I don't want to say who I am, Charity, and therefore it would be quite easy, do you not see, for me to be accepted as Miss Sparling."

"Now why should you want to do that, Miss Vada?" Charity asked in surprise.

"Well, just in case there are any newspaper reporters about," Vada replied. "Supposing they put in the French newspapers that I am staying alone with you at the *Meurice*, it might be copied by the *New York Herald* and then Mama would read about it."

"I never thought of that!" Charity exclaimed. "She'll not approve! I've told you, Miss Vada, she'll not approve!"

"I know," Vada agreed, "and that is why, Charity, I think it's a splendid idea if when we arrive I say that Miss Emmeline Holtz has been detained and will be arriving later and that I am her companion, Miss Nancy Sparling. Can you not see it's a great idea?"

Charity considered the matter for some time.

"Well, I sees little harm in it and I certainly wouldn't like your Mama to know what you're up to. I don't approve, make no bones about that! Miss Sparling should not have suggested it. I'm surprised at her, I am really!"

"I know, Charity, and that is why it will make it so much better if nobody knows who I am."

"Well, I'll not remember to call you Miss Sparling and that's a fact!" Charity said.

"I don't suppose anybody will hear us talking," Vada smiled, "but, if they do, we will just explain that 'Vada' is a nickname, which is exactly what it is."

She saw that Charity looked worried and went on,

"Who is going to ask questions? We know nobody in Paris and Miss Sparling said that she would not give me any introductions because she thought that the French would think it odd, just as Mama would, for me to be staying at an hotel alone."

"You'll be perfectly safe with me, Miss Vada," Charity claimed stoutly.

The journey was long and rather tiring and it was late at night when finally they reached Paris.

Moreover the City was wide awake. No one seemed in need of sleep.

As they drove through the streets from the Railway Station, Vada sat forward to stare out of the carriage window, entranced.

The tall grey houses with their wooden shutters were just what she had expected, but the boulevards were more crowded than she had thought possible.

She could see the crowd of strollers moving slowly past the *café* terraces, where the drinkers of wine had glasses standing before them – amber, green, yellow and mauve in the crude light of the *café* fronts.

The carriage reached the *Place de l'Opera* and Garnier's ornate, fabulous gold and marble building looked like a romantic Palace from a Fairytale.

Vada had asked Nancy Sparling about the Opera House.

"It's brilliant, vulgar, gay, monstrous and imposing," she had replied.

Vada learnt that it had the largest stage in the world.

Now the *voiture* was proceeding down the famous *Rue de la Paix,* the centre of Parisian elegance. It was almost empty at this hour of the night.

They trit-trotted into the *Place Vendôme* where the huge white Trojan column erected to Napoleon Bonaparte towered over the Ministry of Justice and the house where Chopin died.

"It's all so impressive!" Vada enthused aloud.

At the *Hotel Meurice* Vada found that no one was particularly interested in her explanation that Miss Holtz would be coming on later.

They accepted that she was Miss Sparling and she and Charity were shown up to a very large and elaborate suite.

It was just, Vada thought, what her mother would have chosen.

The rooms had thick deep carpets and heavy velvet curtains festooned with fringes and tassels. There were antimacassars on all the damask chairs and there seemed to be more lights than in any room Vada had ever occupied before.

The sitting room was in the centre of the suite with a large bedroom on each side and a smaller one for Charity, besides a host of cupboard wardrobes, bathrooms and *entre-salles*, which made Vada feel their luggage was quite inadequate for all the space provided for it.

Despite the lateness of the hour. Charity insisted on

unpacking quite a number of their trunks, while Vada ordered supper to be brought to the sitting room.

When they had eaten, Vada pushed back her chair and said,

"We are in Paris, Charity. I was so afraid I would never make it!"

"It wouldn't worry me if I never saw these foreign parts again!" Charity replied. "As I says to Madam, I'm getting too old to go gallivanting about the world as if I were eighteen."

"It's an adventure!" Vada said softly.

"Adventures are for those as likes them," Charity answered, "and I don't want you, Miss Vada, involved in anything more daring than a promenade down the *Rue de Rivoli*."

"I expect that is the worst that will happen to me," Vada smiled. "At least I can imagine a dashing dark-eyed Frenchman fighting a duel over me in the *Bois de Boulogne*!"

"Not if I can help it, he won't," Charity said positively and Vada laughed.

All the same she wondered if the Frenchmen she had seen sitting outside the *cafés* would think her attractive.

She was fair with blue eyes, but at the same time very American!

She was not sure if that was an advantage or a disadvantage.

Charity fussed about the bedroom rustling tissue paper long after Vada was undressed, but at last even she seemed to tire and Vada was alone.

She went to the window and pulled back the curtains.

The suite overlooked the *Rue de Rivoli* and beyond it were the gardens of the *Tuileries*.

Vada remembered that the Gardens, now mysterious in the darkness, had been the scene of both bloodshed and heroics.

In 1792, Miss Channing had taught her, Louis XVI had left the *Tuileries* to the invading mob of revolutionaries and his Swiss Guard, whom he had ordered to cease fire, lost two thirds of their numbers while attempting to escape across the Park.

How bald and lifeless such information had seemed when she learnt it, how different to actually see the Gardens and imagine it all happening!

Vada had expected Paris to look bright, but the electricity, which had been introduced three years earlier and had been the beginning of Paris as the *Ville Lumiere* was more exciting even than she had expected.

Everywhere there was the glitter of round shining globes in the street below and a great congregation of them to the right, which Vada was aware was the *Place de la Concorde.*

They looked like glittering golden oranges shining out in the darkness.

'I am in Paris and on my own!' Vada told herself, 'and it's the most exciting thing that has ever happened to me!'

Chapter Three

In the morning, long before Charity was ready, Vada was up, dressed and agitating to be off to see Paris.

"There's no hurry. Miss Vada," Charity kept saying. "I must get these things done first."

"You can leave the rest of the unpacking," Vada said. "If I don't go out, if I don't see the City, I shall go mad, Charity, or I shall go alone!"

This last threat galvanised Charity into action and, hiring an open carriage, Vada told it to drive up the *Champs Élysées*.

It was all she had expected it to be with large and impressive private mansions ranged behind the chestnut trees with their pink and white blooms.

She longed to know who they belonged to, but she was too shy to ask the *cocher* driving the two thin horses that drew the carriage.

She did know, however, that one of the houses and the most impressive had belonged to *La Païva*.

Mrs. Holtz would have been horrified that Vada had even heard of the most notorious *courtesan* of the Second Empire, a Russian born in a Moscow ghetto who was described as 'the greatest *débauchée* of the century'.

But Vada had read a book in French, a language in which her mother was not very proficient, which described the fantastic Palace built for *La Païva* by the wealthy Prince Henckel von Donnersmarch.

It was there that they fostered Prussian interests and, when the Germans entered Paris in March 1871, the Prince, in full uniform, had stood on the steps to watch the troops pass down the *Champs Élysées*.

Vada noticed another palatial house standing in its own garden.

"That's the residence of the Duchesse d'Uzès," the *cocher* suddenly proclaimed, turning round as he spoke.

Americans, he knew, tipped extra for information that should be obtained from a guide.

"Who is the Duchesse?" Vada asked.

"*L'Amazon*," he replied, "owns a pack of twelve hundred hounds for wolf-hunting."

"I had no idea there were wolves in France!" Vada exclaimed. "And who is she?

"*Très belle*," the *cocher* went on, " and *chère amie* of General Boulanger who fought a duel with Prime Minister Floquet."

"Did he win?" Vada asked.

"*Non*, he was wounded in the neck," the *cocher* replied. "Four years ago the General tried to bring back the Royalists. *Voyons*, he failed and committed suicide."

"Poor man!" Charity murmured.

It was not only the width, length and the magnificence of the *Champs Élysées* that Vada had wanted to see, but its numerous sideshows.

There were stalls selling toys and gingerbread, Punch and Judy shows, brightly coloured balloons and children's roundabouts.

There were miniature carriages for tiny tots drawn by goats and already the fashionable Summer Circus was being set up where, Vada learnt, the most snobbish children in Paris would be taken if they behaved themselves.

There were *cafés* outside where top-hatted men and

most elegantly dressed women were already sitting criticising the passers-by.

After the *Rue de la Paix*, Nancy Sparling had told Vada, the *Champs Élysées* was *the* place where one may watch *the Beau Monde* of Paris and see parading the most celebrated representatives of the two great aristocracies.

"How do you mean – two?" Vada had asked.

"Money and blood!" Nancy Sparling replied.

It was too early, Vada thought, to see many of the expensive carriages with magnificent bloodstock carrying the high-born dandies and the famous *courtesans* of whom she had read in books, which would certainly not have been approved of by her mother.

But she thought that she recognised from the description in the social magazines, the Baroness Adolphe de Rothschild, who, beautifully dressed, always rode escorted by two grooms wearing cockaded top hats.

"Oh, Charity, how fascinating it all is!" Vada exclaimed.

All too quickly the carriage carried them away from the *Champs Élysées* and back down the smaller streets with their high grey houses to No. 6, *Rue de la Paix,* the great fashion house of Worth.

Charles Frederick Worth had been born in 1826 in England.

His father was a Solicitor, who gambled away all his money and at the age of eleven young Worth had to leave school and earn his living.

By the time he was thirteen he was a cashier and he later worked in Swan and Edgar's in Piccadilly.

He spent every moment he was free in museums and art galleries. Then before he was twenty he left for Paris, not speaking a word of French and with one hundred francs in his pocket.

He went to work at a silk merchant's and from there began to revolutionise fashion, not only in the design of clothes but in the materials in which they were made.

The splendour of the Second Empire depended to a great extent on the magnificent dresses of its beautiful women, both in Society and out of it.

In 1859 the Empress Eugénie bought her first Worth gown, made of Lyons brocade. From that moment Lyons Silk became a household word and the looms in Lyons increased from fifty-seven thousand to one hundred and twenty thousand.

Vada had read that a man wrote,

"I should not give it as my fixed opinion that Paris is a religious City. No, the men believe in the Bourse and the women in Worth!"

This was a few months before the Empire fell, but Worth, the King of Fashion, kept his throne long after Napoleon III had been deposed.

At sixty-six Charles Worth had a cultured turn of phrase and a poise that made it impossible to believe that he was self-taught.

Faced with the great man, Vada had some explaining to do.

Her mother had written telling Mr. Worth that she wished him to design her daughter's trousseau and ordering him to make a number of gowns ready for her to fit.

Vada had already anticipated that it would be difficult to explain a great number of boxes arriving at the hotel addressed to 'Miss Emmeline Holtz', when she was not supposed to be in residence.

She therefore told Mr. Worth the story that she had concocted about being Miss Holtz's companion.

"Since we are almost identical in height and size," Vada said, "I can easily fit the gowns for her. So, when she does arrive in Paris, there will be little or nothing for her to do but slip them on for you to see her in them."

Mr. Worth laughed and observed,

"It's a new luxury for the very rich, when they have an understudy who can take on all the hard work of being well-dressed!"

He was not very respectful, Vada thought, and perhaps a little more familiar in the way he talked to her than he would have been had he known her to be a rich heiress who was paying for the gowns.

At the same time, when she put on one after another of the half-finished creations that he had designed, there was no doubt that he was delighted with her appearance in them.

"Ravishing! Perfect!" he exclaimed more than once.

Then, as Vada paused in front of a mirror to see herself in a gown of pale pink tulle decorated on the full skirt with bunches of artificial almond blossom, he said,

"I cannot believe, Miss Sparling, that anyone could look more spring-like or indeed more beautiful than you do in that gown."

"*Merci bien*, *monsieur*," Vada replied.

"I can only hope, Miss Sparling," Mr. Worth went on, "that you will have a chance of wearing these gowns yourself one day."

Vada knew that he was anticipating that Emmeline

Holtz would be generous enough to pass on her discarded clothes to her poor companion.

"I hope so," she managed to say a little wistfully.

"Perhaps before we finish I shall be able to find just one little gown for you," Mr. Worth smiled.

And while Vada thanked him profusely she felt a little ashamed of her subterfuge.

There was one last dress ready for her to fit.

A gown of dreams, of white tulle with touches of silver, it was decorated with water lilies, one of Worth's favourite flowers.

Vada put it on. A sash of silver accentuated her tiny waist and there was a wreath of water lilies to wear like a tiara on her fair hair.

She walked from the dressing room into the Salon. Mr. Worth was talking to a gentleman, very elegant in a well-cut frock coat, an emerald tiepin in his exquisitely tied grey cravat.

Vada stood waiting for Mr. Worth to notice her, but the gentleman with him saw her first.

He gave a flattering exclamation of admiration and stood staring, apparently transfixed by her appearance.

A little shyly, Vada advanced.

"Marvellous! Divine! A Goddess from Mount Olympus!" the stranger declared.

Vada reached the Master's side.

"You have, *mademoiselle*, transformed my dream into reality," Mr. Worth said in French.

"Merci, *monsieur*," Vada smiled.

"You are right! She is a dream! I shall never sleep without praying she will be with me in the darkness of the night!" the gentleman cried.

"You have a new admirer. Miss Sparling," Mr. Worth said. "May I introduce the Marquis Stanislas de Guaita?"

Vada curtseyed and the Marquis bowed.

"May I tell you how beautiful you are?" he asked.

Vada bowed her head.

He was handsome, but there was something about him that made her feel embarrassed. He was too suave, too sure of himself.

"If, *monsieur*, you have finished with me," she said to the great designer, "I feel it is time for luncheon."

As she walked back to the dressing room, she knew the Marquis was watching her.

By the time she had changed and returned to the hotel, Vada was feeling really rather tired and glad of the excellent luncheon that they could enjoy in their sitting room.

"Is there nowhere we could have luncheon out together?" she questioned.

"Not for two women alone, Miss Vada," Charity replied. "We can perhaps sit down for a cup of coffee at the *Café de la Paix*, although I'm sure your mother would not approve of it. But not a meal. We can't do nothing like that."

"I have heard how marvellous the French food is in even the smallest *estaminets*," Vada said. "Surely we could go to a very tiny place?"

"I doubt if they'd serve us, Miss Vada," Charity said in an uncompromising tone.

Vada gave a little laugh. She had found a guide book in the sitting room and now she opened it.

"I am greedy!" she exclaimed. "I want to try all the famous French dishes – *Moules en Brochette, Rougets en Papillote, Rognons Flambés, Pieds de Mouton, Rillettes*, snails and frogs!"

"Really, Miss Vada, you make me feel sick!" Charity complained.

"But I want to eat in the great restaurants," Vada cried, turning over the pages of the guide book. "For instance I would like to visit the oldest restaurant in Paris, *La Tour d'Argent* where Sieur Rourteau, ennobled by Henry IV for the excellence of his heron pies, set up business."

"Heron pies? I never heard of eating that great bird!" Charity said.

"It was at the *Tour d'Argent* that forks were first used and coffee and chocolate served for the first time in Paris."

"Fancy that!" Charity remarked, but Vada knew that she was not really interested.

'If only Nancy Sparling was here!' she sighed.

The guide book also told her that *Lapérouse* had once been the mansion of the Comtes de Vruillevert and Voltaire, Balzac and Racine had all eaten there.

'But not Vada Holtz!' she commiserated with herself.

Then she said aloud,

"I suppose I had better write to Mama and tell her about Miss Sparling's accident. She will not receive the letter until after we have left Paris, so that if she is annoyed it will be too late for her to do anything about it!"

"That's right," Charity agreed. "You write to your mother, Miss Vada, I'm just popping out to buy some cotton. There's a button off one of your grey gloves and I saw a shop just round the corner when we were driving here."

She put the glove in a piece of tissue paper.

"If I can't match it there," she went on, "I'll try a little further along the *Rue de Faubourg St. Honoré*. There's a store there I've visited before."

"All right," Vada agreed, "but don't be too long, because there are lots of things I want to see this afternoon."

"You'll wear us both out!" Charity exclaimed.

"Nonsense!" Vada replied. "You have not had to stand on your feet all the morning. You were sitting while I was fitting all those gowns."

Charity did not reply, but picked up her sensible leather handbag and put her short black cape over her shoulders.

"You tell Madam I'm looking after you and you'll come to no harm with me," she said.

Then she went from the sitting room and Vada heard her open the door of the *entre-salle* that led into the main corridor.

She sat for a moment at the large and elaborate desk looking at the leather blotter and ormolu inkpot.

Then she remembered that if Charity was going to the shops she wanted some scent.

On the ship during a storm she had upset a bottle of French perfume she had bought in New York and it was one of the first things she had meant to replace when they arrived in Paris.

Knowing that Charity would not be far down the stairs and that she moved slowly, Vada opened the door of the sitting room and the door onto the passage.

Then she ran down the corridor and started down the wide stairway that led to the vestibule.

Charity had not reached the first floor when Vada caught up with her.

"Charity!" she called.

The old maid turned round.

"What is it, Miss Vada?"

"Please buy me a bottle of my usual scent," Vada said. "A small one will do, for I mean to try some different perfumes, but I hate to be without scent of any sort and you know my bottle was broken on the ship."

"Of course it was," Charity said, "and I meant to make a note of it. Don't you worry, Miss Vada, there's a very good perfume shop just round the corner where Madam used to buy hers. I'll get you a bottle, and when you have time I'll take you there and you can smell all the scents of Araby rolled into one!"

Vada laughed.

"Have you enough money?"

"Yes, plenty," Charity answered.

"Very well then," Vada said, "I will go back to my letter, but don't be too long."

"I can't buy half a dozen things in five minutes!" Charity snapped. "I've only two feet. It'll take me time to get there and time to get back."

Vada laughed.

It was the sort of remark that Charity always made!

Humming a little tune to herself she went back up the stairs which led to the second floor and up again to the third.

She walked along to the door of their suite, which she had left open and, as she entered the *entre-salle* she realised that there was someone in the sitting room.

She thought at first it must be a waiter in spite of the fact that the luncheon had already been cleared away.

Then through the half-open door she saw reflected in the mirror on the mantelshelf the head and shoulders of a man wearing a green coat.

Vada remembered all the stories she had heard of hotel thieves and tricksters who had skeleton keys that could open any door!

With almost a feeling of relief she thought that at the moment at any rate he was not near her jewellery.

Swiftly, her feet moving silently over the thick carpet, she slipped into her bedroom.

When she had come in with Charity before luncheon she had thrown her hat, handbag and gloves down on a chair.

Now she opened the handbag and took out the small pistol that Nancy Sparling had given to her.

She had placed it in her handbag while they travelled and automatically Charity had transferred it from one handbag to the other with all the other things she carried.

The steel of it was cold against Vada's hand and it gave her a confidence that she could deal with the thief, however tough he might be.

It was only later she remembered that the pistol was not loaded. She had left the bullets in her bag.

Walking across the *entre-salle* and into the sitting room, with the pistol held a little in front of her, she said in what sounded even to herself a brave voice,

"Who are you and what are you doing here?"

The man in the green coat was at her desk, which stood on the other side of the room in the window.

He turned round.

He was taller than she had thought in the mirror, broad shouldered and good-looking.

There was also something about his face that Vada could not help thinking would have proclaimed him to be a gentlemen if it had not been for the strangeness of his clothes.

He was wearing a green velvet coat such as she knew that artists wore and a low turned-down collar with a somewhat voluminous black tie.

They stared at each other for a moment across the sitting room and then the stranger said in French,

"*Pardon, mademoiselle*, I must have come to the wrong room."

"I don't believe you!" Vada asserted. "You are a thief. What are you doing with my letters?"

The man looked down at what he held in his hand. He had picked up the small pile of papers that Vada had earlier placed on the desk.

There was a letter from her mother from New York addressed to Miss Emmeline Holtz, which she had not yet opened.

There were the letters that she had read in the train from the hotel and several lists of requirements for her trousseau that her mother had given her before she left.

The man in the green coat stared at them as if in surprise.

Then he put them back on the desk.

"I can only apologise," he said quietly.

"I do *not* accept your apology," Vada replied.

With her pistol still pointed at him she moved towards the bell.

"One moment," he said as she put out her hand to it. "Before you have me arrested, may I tell you that I was not stealing? I am a journalist."

Vada was suddenly very still and her hand fell to her side.

Her eyes were very wide as she repeated in a somewhat uncertain voice,

"A – journalist?"

"*Oui*," the man answered. "I knew this was Mademoiselle Emmeline Holtz's suite and I was curious about the richest young woman in America."

"Mademoiselle is not – here."

"I know that," he answered. "They told me downstairs that she was expected to arrive later. You must be Mademoiselle Sparling?"

"There is nothing – here for you to – write about."

Vada's fear of journalists, which had been drilled into her all her life, made her feel curiously stupid, as if she could not think what to do.

Then she said on an impulse,

"Please – please don't write about Mademoiselle. She does not like it."

"So I have heard," the man in green answered, "and she has managed to keep herself very well hidden from the vulgar gaze of the public."

"How – how do you know that here in Paris?" Vada asked.

"All newspapers have a library in which are filed cuttings, references, articles on any celebrity and anyone of importance," the man replied. "But there is practically nothing about Mademoiselle Holtz, not even a photograph!"

"Then please will you go away and forget that you have been here?" Vada begged.

"I might do that." he replied, "but I am afraid to move with that extremely unpleasant weapon pointing at me."

Vada had almost forgotten that she was holding the

pistol in her hand.

She put it down on the table and said,

"Please go!"

"What shall I write about?" he asked. "Shall I say that Mademoiselle Holtz, as usual, manages to be invisible, but she has an extremely attractive and beautiful companion in the shape of Mademoiselle Sparling?"

"No – please!" Vada said. "Please – please don't write – that."

"Why not?" he enquired.

"Because – "

She tried to think frantically of a reason.

Then she said,

" – it will get me into a great deal of trouble. It might even lose me my job."

The man in green smiled and it gave his face a much younger expression than when he was serious.

At the same time Vada could not help being uncomfortably aware that there was a twinkle in his eyes and she thought that the smile on his lips was faintly mocking.

She reflected that he was not in the least like any journalist she had ever seen in America.

"Which paper do you write for?" she asked, because she could not help being curious about him.

"*La Plume* mostly," he replied.

Her eyes widened.

"You mean the magazine that belongs to the Symbolists?" she enquired.

He smiled.

"What do you know about the Symbolists, *mademoiselle*? Has their fame really reached America?"

"We are not entirely ignorant on the other side of the Atlantic!" Vada said a little stiffly.

Then she knew by the mocking twist of his lips that he was amused by her championship of her country.

"*Bien*! So what do you think Symbolism means?" he enquired.

Vada thought for a moment and then she said,

"I have read that it means freedom of the imagination and unfettered self-expression."

He looked surprised.

"A very good definition."

"You are very patronising!" Vada retorted before she could prevent herself.

Then she realised that this was not at all the conversation that she should be having with a journalist who had crept into her sitting room like a thief.

"Will you go now?" she said in a different tone. "I should not be talking to you like this."

"Why not?" he asked. "After all you are the only person who can tell me something about your employer. Something that no other journalist has managed to elicit about the elusive Mademoiselle Holtz."

"But I thought you said that you would not write about her?" Vada said.

"You were pleading with me, if I remember rightly, not to do so," the man in the green coat said. "If I give you my word of honour that I will not publish anything without your permission, would you allow me to talk to you for a few minutes?"

"I don't – think I ought to do – that."

"She really has you tied up, has she not?" he said mockingly. "What special magic, apart from her money, does Mademoiselle use so that everyone connives in making her more mysterious than the Sphinx?"

Vada gave a little laugh. She could not help it.

"She is not a bit like that."

"What is she like?" the man in green asked.

"You are trying to find things out about her," Vada said accusingly, "and you are doing it in a rather underhand manner. I am not going to talk about Mademoiselle – I cannot!"

"Then I will compromise with you," the man in green said. "We will talk about you."

"No," Vada said with a shy little laugh, "I don't want to talk about myself."

"Then what do you want to talk about?"

"I would like to understand more about Symbolism," Vada answered. "I have read about it in America and it's rather difficult to understand."

"Not really," he replied.

He paused, realising that Vada's eyes were fixed on his face, and said,

"Just as Impressionism represented a revolt against the current standards and conventions in painting, so Symbolism started by representing an attempt to shatter the conventions in poetry."

"It has gone beyond that now, has it not?" Vada asked.

"It has indeed," he replied. "Symbolistic poets have been joined by artists and dramatists and in fact anyone who is interested in the mysterious and spiritual world of the soul and the emotions."

"I think I understand," Vada said. "It means expressing not what one actually sees but what one feels."

"In simple terms that explains it exactly!" the man in

~64~

green smiled.

He looked at her and said,

"Why are you interested in something that must seem very obscure to an American? I cannot believe that 'Miss Moneybags' is concerned in anything like that."

There was something sarcastic and almost scathing in his tone that made Vada say quickly,

"That's unfair! You have never met Mademoiselle Holtz, so why should you condemn her unseen?"

"Prove to me that she is different from the average, rich title-hunting American," he said.

Vada stiffened.

"What do you – mean by – that?" she asked and her voice was hardly above a whisper.

The man in green's eyes seemed to watch her expression as he said,

"I have heard a rumour, of course it may be untrue, that Mademoiselle Holtz was interested in acquiring a title. And an English title at that!"

"Who could have told you such a thing?" Vada asked hotly.

"As a matter of fact," the man in green replied, "my information came from England."

Vada longed to say it was untrue – a complete lie – and yet somehow she could not bring the words to her lips.

Instead she said,

"I thought we agreed that we would not discuss my – my employer?"

"I don't think that there was really much agreement about it," the stranger replied. "At the same time I have told you I am quite prepared to talk about you."

"But I have no wish to talk about myself," Vada

replied. "Will you tell me your name?"

"Pierre Valmont," he replied, "but I am afraid it will mean very little to you."

"You write for *La Plume*?"

"I am part-editor of it, as it happens."

"It's one of the magazines I am determined to buy while I am in Paris," Vada said.

"I will send you a copy or, better still, I will bring it."

"Thank you, I would like that very much."

"That I should bring it to you?"

There was an expression in his eyes that made her feel a little shy.

He had no right to look at her in such a bold appraising manner that it was hardly a compliment.

"I think, Monsieur Valmont, as I am in Paris for such a very short time, we are not likely to meet again."

"What are you going to do while you are in Paris?"

"I want to visit and see – everything I can," Vada answered impulsively, "but I am afraid not all the things I have dreamt about."

"And what would you like to do most?" he asked.

She thought for a moment and then she told the truth.

"For one thing, I would like to hear – the Symbolists. I have read a little of their poetry and seen reviews of it in the American newspapers."

She paused to add wistfully,

"But it is not the same as – actually meeting or listening to a Symbolistic poet."

Pierre Valmont did not speak and she asked,

"Do you write poetry?"

"I have written some," he replied. "It's not very good, but like my fellow poets I have proclaimed my verse at the

~66~

Soleil d'Or."

"Where is that?" Vada asked almost breathlessly.

"It is in the basement of the *café* in the *Place St. Michel.* It's a meeting place started a few years ago by Léon Deschamps, the poet who founded *La Plume."*

"What do the poets do when they go there?"

"Poets, musicians, singers, anyone who is a Symbolist, meet to recite, sing or play to those who will listen."

"It sounds very interesting!" Vada said excitedly.

"Sometimes a Master, like Jean Moréas or Verlaine, will read their latest poem. When the audience is not listening there is much to discuss, views to be exchanged and minds to be stimulated."

"It must be fascinating! Absolutely – fascinating!" Vada said.

She hesitated before she added,

"Do you think it possible that – I could go there? Just to see the poets. I would like to more than – anything in the world!"

"But, of course!" Pierre Valmont replied. "I will take you, if you will go with me."

For a moment there was silence.

It was as if Vada, in what she had been saying, had not realised where the conversation was taking her.

Suddenly his words seemed to pull her up with a jerk.

It was impossible, quite impossible!

Then a voice that was not her own, a being outside herself answered,

"I would be very very – grateful if I could go with – you."

Chapter Four

Vada stood looking into the wardrobe trying to decide which dress she should put on.

It was quite a problem, because, when she had asked Pierre Valmont rather shyly what she should wear, he had replied,

"Anything. You must not expect the Symbolists to be smart."

There was laughter in his eyes and she knew that he was amused at her preoccupation with her appearance.

Equally she did not wish to appear peculiar, as she knew that she would if she wore an evening gown.

There was also the difficulty of Charity.

When Charity returned from shopping, Pierre Valmont had already gone and, if the maid had been a little more perceptive, she would have noticed that Vada was looking flushed and excited.

But after she had told a long tale of the difficulties of finding the right sort of cotton that she required, Vada said casually,

"Oh, by the way, when you were out some friends of Miss Sparling called and I am going out to dinner with them tonight."

Charity had accepted the falsehood without surprise or comment.

Vada could not help feeling that the first lies she had ever had to tell in her life were surprisingly easy.

She did not wish to be anything but open and frank with the old maid she had known since a child. At the same time she could well imagine how horrified Charity would be if she knew the truth.

Even to herself Vada was critical of her behaviour.

How could she have done anything so outrageous as to promise to dine and spend the evening with a man who had not only invaded her sitting room to pick up information about the legendary 'Miss Holtz' but was also a journalist?

And yet, Vada told herself, there was no alternative.

Even if she had met Nancy Sparling's friends, it was doubtful whether any of them would have taken her to the Latin Quarter.

She loved poetry, even though it was something on which her teachers had spent very little time, but there was no one she knew in America who had a good word to say for the Latin Quarter of Paris.

Montmartre had become fashionable. The cabarets there had an increasing appeal for the worldly Cosmopolitan clientele who thought it smart to 'go Bohemian'.

But the Latin Quarter was considered very *outré* and certainly not a place where any American *debutante* would be seen.

In the few American magazines that mentioned it, they stated that it was the centre for the anarchists, who had been making a stir in all the Capital Cities of the world.

The most extreme and revolutionary artists and students who were denounced fervently by everyone who was traditional and conventional were, they reported, to be found on the Left Bank.

Yet somehow Vada found herself fascinated by the Latin Quarter.

She had learnt that it was the natural home for all the

young provincials and foreigners who came to Paris to write poetry, paint masterpieces and try to revolutionise the world.

But never, she thought excitedly, had she ever imagined that she would one day have the chance of going there.

She was rather doubtful as to whether Nancy Sparling would have taken her even to Montmartre and she thought as she started to change her gown that she would never have dared to suggest that they might make the trip to the *Soleil d'Or*.

'What would Mama say?' Vada asked herself.

Slim and elegant in her pretty lace-trimmed underclothes, she saw herself reflected in the long mirror on the wardrobe door.

'Whatever Mama might say,' she answered herself, 'this is my last chance, my only chance, of going to such a place or of meeting a poet.'

As a Duchess she could visualise all too clearly that even to speak of the Latin Quarter would cause raised eyebrows and undoubtedly evoke a rebuke from her husband, if he was the sort of person she expected him to be.

She could imagine how his mother, the Dowager Duchess, might look down her aristocratic nose at some of the more gaudy and vulgar sights on Long Island.

If she could be shocked by America, how much more would she be shocked by the Latin Quarter of Paris and the Bohemians that Vada expected to find there?

There was still the problem of her gown.

Irrepressibly she wanted to look her best, but at the same time not to proclaim herself a rich American amongst people who were finding it difficult to find enough money to eat while they expressed what was in their souls.

Finally she chose one of the dresses that she wore at home at teatime.

It was of rose-silk draped round the full skirt and trimmed with a muslin fichu round the neck. It was caught at the breast with a small bunch of rosebuds.

It was simple because she had worn it for over a year and only now when she was supposedly grown up was she allowed to appear in more sophisticated and extravagantly decorated gowns that were the fashion.

But the tightly moulded bodice revealed the curves of her tip-tilted breasts and her neck rose white and graceful from the soft muslin.

She swept her hair back from her oval forehead and twisted it into a big coil low at the back of her head.

It made her look more than ever like one of Charles Gibson's lovely American women.

"What are you wearing that old thing for, Miss Vada?" Charity asked when she came into the room. "I only brought it with us because I thought it would be useful on board ship."

"I don't want to look too smart tonight," Vada answered truthfully.

"All the same, Miss Vada, I wouldn't want the French looking down on you. They always think we Americans have no taste and I should have thought that dress was far too simple and ordinary for a dinner in Paris."

"It is what I want to wear," Vada said firmly.

"It suits you, I'm not saying it doesn't," Charity went on, "but then most things suit you, Miss Vada. Why, even Mr. Worth said to me this morning while you were trying on his gowns, '*she is lovely, that is what she is! Lovely!*' And I wasn't going to argue with him!"

"Thank you, Charity," Vada laughed.

When she was ready with only a chiffon scarf as a wrap because it was warm, she waited apprehensively for a pageboy to tell her that Pierre Valmont was downstairs.

"You must not come to the sitting room," she had said to him. "My maid, or rather Miss Holtz's maid, is with me and will think it strange there is not a lady with you."

"Do you think it strange?" he asked in an amused voice.

"I-I don't mind if it is," Vada had replied. "I do so want to see your friends – the Symbolists."

He had no idea, she thought, what a tremendous gesture of independence her acceptance of his invitation was.

Never had she been anywhere without a chaperone.

Never as far as she could remember in her whole life had she been able to choose an entertainment for herself, whether it was the theatre, a party or even a visit to some tourist sight.

Everything had always been planned and arranged and she had just been taken from place to place or stuffed with knowledge that was thought right for her as if she was a puppet.

What was more, Vada was certain that her life with her future husband would follow the same pattern of her life with her mother.

Mrs. Holtz's mother had been English and she had visited her English relatives many times.

The ordinary pattern of behaviour in the Holtz home was therefore much on English lines.

Vada could remember even her father rebelling occasionally.

Once he had said,

"I am not interested what the English do or do not do! I am a *goddamned* American and that is how I'll behave!"

She could not remember now what had provoked this outburst, but she remembered that her mother walked about with pursed lips and sulked until he apologised.

An apology made all the more acceptable because with it came a diamond bracelet in a Tiffany box.

How, Vada asked herself, in the circumstances, could she refuse what seemed a Heaven-sent opportunity in the person of Pierre Valmont to see and hear what she had always believed would be the impossible?

At last she was told that he was downstairs and escorted by the pageboy resplendent in shining buttons, she found him in one of the lounges on the ground floor.

His green velvet coat and the flowing black silk tie seemed out of place amongst the potted plants, the heavy Genoese velvet upholstered sofas and damask-covered walls, interspersed with long gilt-framed mirrors.

Vada felt shy as she walked towards him, knowing that his eyes were on her and feeling that he was perhaps criticising her appearance.

Because he did not speak, she said the first thing that was in her mind,

"I was so afraid that you would forget to call for me!"

Pierre Valmont smiled.

"Did you really believe that I could forget anything so important? Perhaps I should tell you that I was counting the minutes."

Vada laughed.

"If you did, I should not believe you. It is too obviously the type of compliment one would expect to hear from a Frenchman!"

"Then shall I say it in English?" he suggested. "I was so looking forward to our next meeting!"

"You speak English!" she exclaimed in delight.

"I am sure I don't speak it as fluently as you speak French!"

"Now that's a compliment I appreciate," she said. "It's almost worth the tears I spent over those horrible complicated verbs!"

"The result is most impressive and wholly enchanting!"

Again Vada felt a little shy.

Somehow, now that they were speaking in English, she felt embarrassed as she had not done when they talked together in French.

"I thought," Pierre Valmont said, "that we might first have something to eat together. Although I can recommend the atmosphere of the *Soleil d'Or*, I cannot say the same of the food."

"That would be lovely!" Vada said. "I wanted so much to go to a restaurant in Paris, but I felt I might never have the opportunity."

"Why not?" he enquired.

"I did not think they would serve two women alone."

"There are plenty of places where it would not matter," he replied. "Of course, if you carried an American flag, any restaurant would understand!"

She knew that he was mocking her and she countered defiantly,

"You mean that the Americans are so outrageous that

no one would be surprised at anything they would do?"

"I would rather use the word 'courageous'," he said quietly, "and that is what you are being tonight, so come along. I have a lot to show you."

She went with him to the door of the hotel.

The Commissionaire called them a *voiture* and on Pierre Valmont's instruction had the hood pulled back.

"It's a warm night," he said, "and I want you to see Paris, especially when we cross the Seine."

"You understand so well what I want to do," Vada replied. "This is what I have often dreamt about, but then I thought that it was a dream that would never come true."

"Is Paris really such a Paradise for young American women?" Pierre Valmont asked.

"It's not only the City itself," Vada said. "I think it is because it expresses for everyone – freedom, a breaking away from restrictions and everything that has become over-conventional and static."

He turned sideways in the carriage to gaze at her.

"You know, you are a very exceptional person. I am used to hearing those sorts of phrases from young men who trek to Paris because they believe that they can find here the chance of expressing what they feel."

He paused, his eyes on her face as he continued,

"It's not what I expected to hear from a woman, especially not from one who looks like you."

"What have my looks to do with it?" Vada asked.

"You are very lovely!" he said, "as hundreds of men must have told you already."

She did not answer.

How could she explain to him that no man would have dared say such things to Miss Emmeline Holtz in the hearing of her mother?

Since she had grown up there had been practically no occasion when either her mother or someone else had not been within hearing distance.

Vada was saved from making a direct reply to his words, which had made her flush a little so that the colour had crept up her white skin.

There was so much to look at, so much to exclaim about. On what must have been Pierre Valmont's instructions, the carriage carried them along the *Rue de Rivoli* into the *Place de la Concorde*.

The fountains were playing and the water thrown high into the air caught the last rosy gleam of the setting sun.

Behind them the pink and white blossoms on the chestnut trees in the *Champs Élysées* looked like candles on a Christmas tree and the great height of the Luxor Obelisk was silhouetted against the sky.

"This was *La Place de la Révolution*," Vada said almost beneath her breath.

"Here Louis XVI was guillotined in 1792 saying, '*I die innocent. May my blood consolidate the happiness of the French people*'," Pierre Valmont added.

It was as if he was playing a game with her, Vada thought, as she wanted it played.

"How many people were guillotined here?" she asked.

"Over fifteen hundred including Marie Antoinette, Madame du Barry, Danton and Charlotte Corday."

"Do you think their ghosts haunt it?"

"No, we shall find them in more amusing places."

"Such as?"

"The places I will show you, if you stay long enough in Paris."

Vada sighed – how in one week could she do everything she wanted to do, even with Pierre Valmont's help?

At the far corner of the *Place de la Concorde* the carriage turned left and drove along the side of the Seine moving like molten silver beneath its numerous bridges.

"Could anything be more enchanting?" Vada cried in delight.

"Nothing!" Pierre Valmont agreed, but he was looking at her.

Suddenly just ahead of them loomed the esoteric grey beauty of *Notre Dame* as they crossed the Seine.

"Ever since the early Middle Ages," Pierre Valmont said, "poets have been living amongst the students on the Left Bank. Unfortunately Baron Haussmann drove the *Boulevard St. Michel* through the centre of the district and many picturesque old streets and houses were destroyed."

"That is vandalism!" Vada exclaimed.

"That is what we think," Pierre Valmont replied, "but he was not able to sweep away the spirit of the Latin Quarter. It is still the same – free with its rebellious camaraderie and always, as you will see, very lively."

The houses were old and the streets narrow.

Then they drew up at a small, unimpressive little restaurant, which seemed almost dwarfed by the height of the houses above and on each side of it.

Inside it was not in the least what Vada had expected.

There was sawdust on the floor and the tables were in little alcoves, partitioned off with wooden sides, not unlike horseboxes in a stable.

A buxom lady, who Vada guessed was the proprietor's wife, was presiding over a small bar at one end.

Through an open door behind her there was a glimpse of the kitchen where *Monsieur le Patron* himself, wearing the high white cap of a chef, was chopping away at what appeared to be a very large carcass.

Pierre Valmont waved to Madame and escorted Vada to a table in a corner of the room.

Here, on a clean red-checked tablecloth, obviously washed a thousand times, was the menu written out for them in spidery writing which Vada had great difficulty in deciphering.

"Will you order for me?" she asked Pierre Valmont.

"Do you want to try their specialities?" he asked.

"Oh – please!" she replied.

He gave the order to an elderly waiter, discussing the food with him course by course as if it was of paramount importance that they should understand exactly what they were eating.

Finally, after what to Vada seemed an endless discussion, he ordered a bottle of wine and then sat back on the wooden settle to look at her.

"This is hardly the *Grand Véfour* or *Lapérous*," he said, "but the food is excellent. Monsieur Louis is a genius in his own way."

Vada looked round the small restaurant with its undecorated walls, its primitive furniture and the bottles stacked up behind the bar.

Pierre Valmont watched her.

"Well?"

"It's fascinating!"

"That is what I hoped you would say. Madame and Monsieur both get up at five o'clock every morning to go to *Les Halles* to choose the very best materials for their craft. Their clients are not rich, but everyone who comes here has an appreciation of what food should taste like."

He pointed out to Vada where there was a huge block of golden butter fresh from the country and cheeses that had been chosen because they were exactly ripe.

He showed her the *Carte des Vins* which, although it was short, consisted of wines which were all, he explained, of exceptional quality.

"I thought everyone in this district was very poor," Vada said. "How can they afford such things?"

"The French consider food one of the most important arts of living," Pierre Valmont explained, "and a Frenchman will go anywhere to find good food. This may be the Latin Quarter, but gourmets from all over Paris will come here to eat what Monsieur Louis provides."

A few minutes later Monsieur Louis himself came out from the kitchen. Pierre Valmont shook him by the hand and introduced him to Vada.

Because she knew it was expected, she too shook him by the hand.

"Mademoiselle is American," Pierre Valmont explained, "and this is her first visit to a French restaurant."

"Then I am honoured!" Monsieur Louis said. "I can only hope, *m'selle,* you will not be disappointed."

"I am sure I will not be," Vada replied.

Monsieur went back to the kitchen and Pierre put his elbows on the table and rested his chin in his hands.

"Now," he said, "I expect to be re-paid for the dinner you are going to eat."

"How?" Vada asked.

"By your telling me a little about yourself," he answered. "I am very curious."

"I think that's unfair," she said. "You know I don't want to talk about myself, nor Miss Holtz, and it is going to be very difficult to refuse as you are being such a very generous host."

She paused for a moment and then continued anxiously,

"You must not think it rude of me, but can you really afford to bring me here this evening?"

"If I reply that I cannot," Pierre Valmont asked, "what will you do?"

"I will, of course, offer to pay my half."

He laughed.

"From a French woman that would be insulting, but from an independent American girl I suppose it is a practical solution."

"Then you will let me?"

"I should not only be furious at the suggestion, but I should take you home immediately you have finished your dinner."

"That is the worst threat you could possibly hold over me," Vada said. "You know how much I am looking forward to this evening."

"This afternoon you asked me if I wrote poetry. I am now asking you the same question."

Vada looked down.

"I have – tried," she said, "but only – secretly."

"Why secretly?" he enquired.

"Because my mother and those who taught me – would not understand."

"Who taught you? Did you go to school?"

"No, of course not!"

"Then you had a Governess, a withered spinster who

had no knowledge of life outside the schoolroom and made learning an intolerable bore!"

Vada laughed.

"No! It was not as bad as that! But you sound as if you have had experience of Governesses."

"I have met the species!" Pierre Valmont admitted. "They are the same the world over, in Paris, England and Germany and I imagine in America too!"

Vada did not speak and he went on,

"That is why it surprises me that you speak French as fluently and as thoughtfully as you do. Most girls of your age are stereotyped, turned out in a universal mould."

He hesitated, and then he said,

"Perhaps because you have had to earn your own living, even though I imagine it's rather a comfortable post you enjoy now, you are different."

"Miss Holtz is a friend," Vada said quickly.

She felt that she was cheating in some way by pretending to be poor and in need of employment.

"You are still subservient," he said. "Is she kind to you?"

"Of course."

"But she is your employer, someone who gives you orders to do this and to do that and, of course, is prepared to pay for it."

"Is money so very important?" Vada asked.

"It certainly is when you are Miss Holtz," Pierre Valmont replied. "Think what it must mean to realise that with millions and millions of American dollars you can buy any man you fancy for a husband. A French Duke, a German Prince, an English Marquis or indeed an English Duke for that matter!"

Vada played with a fork that she had picked up from the table.

"Do you – think that Miss Holtz or any – other woman for that matter in her position – has much choice?" she asked hesitatingly.

"You mean that such marriages are arranged by the parents on either side?" Pierre Valmont asked. "That is what happens to the poor little French *demoiselles*! A French husband will count up every *sou* of the dowry to make certain it is worthwhile giving his august name to some fledgling who has just left the schoolroom. At the same time he makes quite sure that his attractive and expensive mistress makes him the envy of his contemporaries."

Vada was very still.

"Does that – always happen with a – French marriage?" she asked.

"But, of course." Pierre Valmont replied. "A Frenchman has a mistress as he has a horse, a carriage, a *garçonnière*, what you would call a bachelor apartment. It is all part of his set-up."

"And an – Englishman?"

Vada had difficulty in saying the words.

Pierre Valmont saw that her fingers holding the fork were suddenly tense.

"Are you worrying about 'Miss Moneybags'?" he asked. "Let me assure you, the English are usually far more circumspect. What is more, few Englishmen can afford a wife and a mistress at the same time."

Vada felt a sudden relief sweep over her.

"I was only – wondering," she said.

"You make me think," Pierre Valmont went on, "that those rumours about Miss Holtz seeking an English title have some truth in them after all."

"But why should you think so?"

"Because," he replied, "it is surely very obvious that someone in her position will give the English Marriage Market a close scrutiny and buy the best!"

"You make it sound – horrible!" Vada said indignantly.

Pierre Valmont shrugged his shoulders.

"I am being practical," he answered.

"You make it all so commercial."

"But that is exactly what it is," he argued. "Incidentally, you might tell your friend that there are only two Nobilities in Europe she should think worth considering. The German and the English."

"Why?" Vada asked, recalling that this was very like a conversation she had already had with her mother.

"Because in France the really old families seldom marry outside their blood and both here and in Italy all the sons of a Prince are Princes, or Comte are Comtes, so there are now too many of them and titles mean very little."

"In Germany and England it is – different?"

"Yes, since only the eldest son or other next of kin, succeeds to the title. That is why, where your friend is concerned, she will find those two countries will produce far the most eligible and suitable husbands."

"I think you are assuming far too much," Vada said sharply.

Then, as if she suddenly realised who she was talking to, she said,

"You promise me – you swear that you would not sell anything we have talked about to the newspapers?"

He saw the fear in her eyes and, putting out his hand,

laid it over hers.

"Listen, Miss Sparling," he said, "I promise you one thing, in fact if it pleases you, I will swear it. Nothing we say tonight will ever appear in print. I am off duty!"

He smiled as he spoke and Vada found herself smiling back at him.

"Thank – you," she murmured.

His hand was still holding hers. His fingers were warm, strong and somehow reassuring.

Then he released her.

"And what is more," he went on, "I promise never to embarrass you or involve you in any situation for which you could be reprimanded by your employer. That, according to my code of behaviour, would be unforgivable."

"Thank you again."

"And now let's enjoy ourselves," Pierre Valmont said. "Because we are going to have a very informal evening, I suggest we drop all formality. '*Mademoiselle*' sounds stiff. 'Miss Sparling' in English is what my old nurse used to call 'a mouthful'!"

Vada laughed.

It was an expression that Charity used too.

"It seems very – unconventional on such short – acquaintance," she said a little hesitatingly.

"I think there are people in the world one has known for a long time, even if you have only just met them," Pierre Valmont remarked.

"Has that happened to you too?" Vada asked. "It has – happened to me and I thought it was just – imagination."

"It was certainly not imagination when we met again," Pierre Valmont said.

"Met again?" she questioned.

"Perhaps it was many centuries ago," he said. "Perhaps because you love Paris you were here in the reign of the Sun King. I can somehow imagine you gracing Versailles, dancing at the *Tuileries* and hunting through the forests in search of wild boar."

"Did you guess – I love riding?" Vada asked.

"I can guess a great many things about you," he said, "and I am convinced, although I have no logical reason for it, that I know a great many more."

Vada felt a strange feeling within her when he spoke to her like that.

She could not explain it, she only knew that it was a delight beyond anything that she had ever known to talk to Pierre Valmont and to know that he was listening to what she had to say!

She also hoped, although she was not quite sure, that there was admiration in his eyes.

They talked of painters.

"If you would come to my studio I will show you some Symbolistic paintings," Pierre Valmont said.

"I would love that," Vada answered. "Do you live near here?"

"Quite near," he replied.

"Can I come there tonight?" Vada asked eagerly.

He paused as if in surprise before he replied,

"Of course, I shall be honoured."

When dinner was over, a delicious delectable meal so light and yet with such undercurrents of taste that it was different from anything Vada had ever had before, they thanked Monsieur and Madame Louis and then walked out into the narrow street.

"The *Soleil d'Or* is not far," Pierre Valmont said, "and if you put your arm in mine, I will protect you from being run over by the *cochers*, who often drive too fast through these narrow streets."

Immediately Vada linked her arm in his. She thought as they walked along how shocked and horrified her mother would be if she could see her.

What was more she had given Pierre Valmont permission to call her by her Christian name!

"I am not called 'Nancy' at home," she had explained to him a little hesitatingly, "but 'Vada'. That is the name I called myself when I was a child."

"I like that much better," he said, "it suits you. It sounds brave, valiant and perhaps discerning, all of which you are."

"I am not really brave," Vada answered, thinking how easily she gave in to her mother as if she had no will of her own.

"I think courage is relative. Sometimes we think we are cowards and then we find that we have an inner resource and determination, which makes us behave with the utmost bravery on unexpected occasions."

'That is what I am being now,' Vada thought to herself. 'Brave! Brave to grasp at this opportunity when it presents itself, brave to let a man of whom I know nothing take me about Paris. Brave to – trust him.'

And yet it seemed to her that there was no real bravery in it, for she knew irrefutably that Pierre was trustworthy.

To reach the basement room of the *Soleil d'Or*, Vada found that they had to pass through a *café* and the largely deserted ground floor, where there were only a few locals playing cards.

They went down a narrow flight of steps behind the bar to the basement.

Pierre had already told her that, while the *Soleil d'Or* was open every night, on every second Saturday there was a *Soirée de la Plume*, which had been inaugurated by Léon Deschamps, who had founded the magazine.

As they lingered over their coffee Pierre had explained how most other magazines only represented a single school or tendency.

La Plume was open to them all.

It was some months after the foundation of the magazine that Deschamps had the idea of bringing his collaborators and artists together.

"At first we met at another *café*," he went on. "Then, as the numbers grew and grew, I joined him in his enterprise and together we hired the basement room at the *Soleil D'Or*."

"People pay to go there?" Vada asked.

He shook his head.

"No subscription is demanded and only politics are excluded from these meetings which are now attended by all the intellectual youth of Paris."

As she reached the bottom of the stairs, Vada found herself in a large, low-ceilinged, smoke-filled room.

The walls were decorated with rough sketches, many of them by Gauguin, whom Pierre had told her was considered a Symbolist by his contemporaries.

There were also portraits of contributors to *La Plume*, scribbles and signatures on pieces of paper, cards and amongst them some very lovely paintings which she would have liked to own.

At the end of the room there was a rough stage on

which, at the moment she and Pierre entered, someone was playing a tinny piano.

All around were sitting the poets, artists and the students she had come to see.

The room was not yet full, but it was filling up all the time.

Those that were there turned round to shout a greeting to Pierre, to wave to him and to stare with a certain amount of curiosity, Vada realised, at herself.

Many of the occupants of the small tables, on which there were large mugs of beer or very small glasses of wine, were wearing capes and the wide-brimmed felt hats that she knew were fashionable in the Latin Quarter.

There seemed to her already a great number of people present and Pierre had already explained to her that they could squeeze as many as two hundred into the basement.

"You will see," he said before they left the restaurant, "that all the various groups and coteries will be represented. 'Parnassians', 'brutalists', 'decadents', 'instrumentists', 'Kabbalists' and the anarchists will all be there."

"Anarchists?" Vada exclaimed in horror.

"I promise you, you will not be blown up!" he laughed. "They are a definite part of Paris life and as such we don't exclude them from our *soirées*."

Vada had expected to feel that the Symbolists and their friends were friendly, but she soon learnt that one of the virtues of the place was that everyone immediately felt at home.

There was a friendliness and camaraderie that she could not explain, but which she could feel very strongly.

There was also an excitement, a kind of youthful

vitality and vigour that made it very different from the family meetings or groups of people she had met in America.

They had hardly seated themselves at a table near the small stage before someone rose to recite a poem.

It was not a very good poem, Vada thought, and yet it received a kindly hearing and there was a certain amount of applause before the poet, obviously delighted that he had been given a chance to express himself, sat down again.

Then a man played a guitar and another read a rather dull piece of prose, which he had composed in honour of some artist of whom Vada had never heard.

The atmosphere was becoming thick. Men and women passed constantly amongst the tables, which already seemed packed to overflowing.

It was very hot and tobacco smoke seemed to cover everyone with a grey cloud.

Whenever no one was performing the voices rose and fell like the waves of the sea, arguing, discussing theories of verse, criticising or extolling each other!

It seemed to Vada that the sharpness of their wits could almost be felt physically in the air!

All the time, the *soucoupes* or small saucers on which the drink was brought piled up before them on the marble tables.

Then, after Vada and Pierre had been there for about an hour, there was a sudden stir as a man came into the room and those nearest the stairs began to shout a welcome.

"It is Paul Verlaine," Pierre said. "I hoped he would be here this evening."

Vada had heard of Paul Verlaine, the poet who had

become a living legend in Paris in the 1880s.

She had read in one of the American magazines that had denounced him scathingly that his life was pathetic. He had been in a prison hospital, he was always ill and an alcoholic.

He had lost his wife and was worn out in the ceaseless search for what few francs he could obtain from publishers and editors to live on.

And yet what Vada had heard about him fascinated her, as it fascinated the young men crowded into the basement, who were greeting him as their leader and Master.

Son of an Army Officer and a respectable, well-to-do mother, all his life Verlaine had been a double personality, a bourgeois and a Bohemian!

His wife went further and claimed that he was 'Prince Charming and the Beast'.

At eighteen he already showed signs of alcoholic tendencies which were inherited and it moved him to outbursts of homicidal violence.

Yet Pierre told Vada,

"He has brought French poetry as close as it will ever come to music."

Verlaine came up the room and Pierre rose to hold out his hand.

"I am glad, Paul, you could come this evening." he said and then introduced Vada.

Verlaine murmured some response and sat down at a table where four young men seemed to envelop him with their attentions.

His face was worn and tired. His long coat gave him the appearance of a poor old street singer and a worn felt hat covered his head until he took it off and Vada saw that he was bald.

Only a yellow silk scarf broke the grey monotony of his sad down-at-heel exterior, but with his eyes half closed and his thin hands trembling she had the impression that he lived in his dreams without heeding what was happening to him outside.

"I hope he will recite for us," Pierre said.

As he spoke, Paul Verlaine rose to his feet and dragged a piece of battered paper from the torn pocket of his long coat.

It was obvious that his companions had persuaded him to perform and they helped him up onto the small stage.

Someone struck an octave on the piano to command attention, but there was no need.

The whole room was suddenly hushed and there was that pregnant expectant silence which only the greatest of artists can inspire.

The poem Verlaine recited was simple, exquisitely written and perfect in its construction.

But it was not the words that mattered, it was the feeling behind them and the emotion which was aroused in those who listened.

It was a long poem, but Verlaine's voice was mesmeric and it seemed to Vada, when he had finished, that one line remained fixed in her memory and repeated itself within her,

"*L'amour toujours monte comme la flamme.*"

'Love always rises like a flame,' she translated and found herself wondering if that was true.

She knew so little about life and yet vaguely she

understood that this was what all these people congregated in the basement room were searching for.

Love of life, love of God, love of themselves, the love that inspired and animated everything on earth.

Love – the common denominator of all!

When Verlaine had sat down amidst tumultuous applause, Vada wondered if it would be possible for anyone to follow him.

No poet could emulate the poem that had made their hearts vibrate with strange and enchanted emotions.

Then Pierre rose to speak to four men sitting at a table at the other side of the room.

Obediently they went to the platform and, as they produced their instruments, Vada thought to herself that only music could follow words as moving as Verlaine's.

One man sat down at the piano, another played the violin, the third an accordion, the fourth, oddly enough, a mouth organ.

It was a strange and unusual orchestra and yet, when they began to play, Vada could understand why Pierre had asked them to do so.

She was listening to the music of the greatest musical Symbolist of them all – Wagner.

She had heard his music once or twice, although her mother did not really consider him suitable for young girls.

Now in this packed smoke-filled room it seemed to Vada from the very first chords that she felt herself plunging into infinite space.

Little by little as Wagner expanded his theme she found herself in ecstatic adoration of what he expounded and she experienced a Divine sense of space.

It was almost impossible to put into words and yet she

knew that Wagner had dragged her small, rather frightened personality out from its hiding-place and made her acknowledge the wonder of immense horizons of almost inconceivable limit.

Without realising what she was doing, as the music following upon Verlaine's verse moved Vada tremendously, she put her hand into Pierre's.

She was not conscious whether his hand was already there waiting for her or whether she sought it.

She only knew that she wanted the comfort of not being alone and she wanted to feel that he felt as she did, that this was a tremendous moment of individual development.

Then, when the music finally swept to a crescendo to finish so that one felt almost deprived because it was ended, she turned her eyes to his and knew without asking him in words that he understood.

He rose to his feet and she knew that he would not ask her to stay any longer in case the wonder of what she had experienced would be spoilt.

They moved from the room, Pierre being hailed on all sides, hands going out to grasp his, a dozen slaps on his shoulder.

The night air seemed fresh and fragrant after the thickness of the atmosphere in the basement.

Pierre put his hand under Vada's elbow and they walked along in silence.

'Words are unnecessary,' she thought. 'He knows what I am feeling and I know that he feels the same.'

She did not even wonder where he was taking her until suddenly she found herself standing on the banks of the Seine looking out onto the silver river.

Just in front of them, silhouetted against the star-strewn sky, was the huge dark outline of *Notre Dame*.

There were lights reflected in the shimmering water. Passing very slowly down the river was a barge, its red and green lights gleaming in the darkness.

Vada drew a deep breath.

"It's so – unbelievably enchanting!"

They were the first words she had spoken since Verlaine had recited his poem.

"And so are you, my sweet," Pierre said.

She was surprised both by his words and by the deepness of his voice.

Then, as she turned to look at him, his arms were around her and he drew her close.

For a moment Vada did not understand what he was about to do.

Before she could think, before it seemed to her that she could breathe, his lips were on hers.

She was too surprised, too astonished to move.

Then, before she could struggle against him, she felt a sensation akin to, yet still more wonderful than what she had felt as she listened to Wagner.

It was a wonder and a rapture such as she had never known.

A streak of lightning that shot through her body and left her so weak that she was unable to struggle, but could only surrender herself to the inestimable glory of it.

It seemed to her as if not only Pierre's lips possessed her but the beauty of the evening.

The river, *Notre Dame* and the starlit sky were all part of herself and therefore a part of him.

They all merged into the warm wonder of his kiss until

it seemed to Vada as if no one could feel so intensely and not die of the joy of it.

She knew very vaguely, far away at the back of her mind, that she should make some effort, but she was no longer herself.

Vada Holtz had ceased to exist.

She was caught up in the mystery of creation, part of the intensity and mystery of life itself.

This she knew was living!

This was coming alive!

Then a flame rose within her, burning its way through her body from the very depths of her soul.

Chapter Five

"*Ma belle, ma petite*," Pierre murmured hoarsely.

Then he was kissing Vada again, kissing her until everything whirled about her and she could no longer think.

The sound of horses' hoofs on the cobblestones and the wheels of a *voiture* rattling past them seemed like an intrusion from another world.

Pierre released her.

"Come," he said, 'let's go somewhere quiet."

He put his hand under her arm as he had done before and they walked away from the Seine through a narrow winding street.

They moved without speaking and somehow there were no words that seemed adequate or possible at the moment.

Pierre stopped.

He pushed open the door of a tall narrow house and drew Vada into a small square hall.

There was a steep staircase ascending into the darkness above, which was barely relieved by one flickering oil lamp on the landing.

They climbed up four storeys. Pierre opened a door with a key that he took from his pocket and Vada entered what she realised was his studio.

It was a large room running across the whole length of the building.

At one end of it there was a window stretching from floor to ceiling and, while Pierre lit a lamp, she instinctively walked towards it.

It was as if all Paris lay beneath her as she gazed over the grey roofs of hundreds of buildings. In the distance there were lights looking like stars that had fallen from the Heavens above.

She stood contemplating the loveliness of it for a few moments and then she turned round.

Pierre had lit a lamp, which was casting a soft golden glow over the room.

There was an easel, brushes, a palette, canvases and a number of unidentifiable bottles.

All the walls were covered with pictures, some with frames, some without, some painted in oils or charcoal, others just pen-and-ink sketches.

Vada looked around in delight.

"This is exactly what I thought a studio would look like!"

"It is tidier than most!" Pierre replied.

At one end there was a huge divan bed on which a flame scarlet silk cover made a patch of glowing colour.

Vada glanced at it as if in surprise.

Pierre walked towards her.

"One day," he said, "I will show you the pictures and explain to you what they are all about. Now I am interested in only one thing."

"What is that?" she enquired.

"*You!*"

He put his arms around her.

"You are more beautiful, far more desirable than any picture!"

She felt herself quivering because of the depth in his voice and because he had drawn her close to him again.

Instinctively she looked up to see the expression in his

~97~

face and his lips were on hers.

He kissed her wildly and with a passion that was different from his kiss by the Seine.

His lips seemed to draw her heart from her body and make it his.

"You are so sweet, so soft, so adorable!" he murmured.

Then his lips were on her neck and the sensation was different from how she had felt before.

It was a rapture, a joy, it made her whole body quiver and yet she could hardly breathe.

She felt something primitive rise inside her, which was as wild as Pierre's kisses and yet it was still part of the magic of the music and Verlaine's poetry.

He drew her close and even closer –

Suddenly Vada realised that he was undoing the buttons at the back of her gown.

She made a little movement to free herself, but found that she was completely captive in his arms.

He was stronger than she had thought and she felt ineffective and weak as if she could not escape him and he was overpowering her.

"No – please – no!"

He did not seem to hear her.

"Pierre – no – I – "

He had pulled her dress aside and was kissing her neck and shoulders with hot burning kisses that seemed to sear their way through her skin.

Yet at the same time she felt as if he still possessed her mouth.

"Please – " she pleaded and then in a sudden fear, " – you are – frightening me – I am – afraid!"

It was the cry of a child and Pierre raised his head to look down into the wide darkness of her eyes.

He searched her face.

"You – you must not – do that – it is wrong!"

Pierre stiffened, but he still held her in his arms.

"What are you saying to me?" he asked.

"Y-you must not – kiss me like – that. You must not – undo my gown. It – it's – wrong! I am – sure it is – wrong!"

"Why?"

"I don't know – but you must not – "

"I want you."

"I don't – understand."

"You came here," he said.

"I wanted – to see your – studio."

"And you did not think that was wrong?"

"No – but I think – perhaps – now I should – go away."

She felt shy and uncertain.

She was conscious of her bare shoulders and that Pierre was looking at her in a strange manner.

Suddenly Vada thought of her mother!

She put up her hands to push him from her and he let her go. She took several steps away from him, putting up her hands to the neck of the dress to fasten the buttons that he had undone.

He stood still, watching her, a flickering fire in his eyes.

Then he said almost sharply,

"Come here! I want to ask you something."

Slowly, her eyes apprehensive, she obeyed him and, when she was close at his side, he put out his hand to her chin.

He turned her face up to his so that the light was on it.

"Tell me, Vada," he said in his deep voice, "have you ever been to a man's rooms before?"

"N-no – never."

"But you have been – kissed?"

The question was somehow an accusation.

Vada's eyes flickered and the colour rose in her cheeks.

"Only by – you."

"Then why did you let me?"

"I did – not think – and I did not – know – "

"Know what?"

"That a – kiss could be so – wonderful! Like the – poetry and the – music we have just – heard."

His fingers were still under her chin and he was still looking into her eyes.

"You swear to me that is the truth?"

"I – swear it! Why should I – lie?"

"You are so young!" he said, as if to himself. "So ridiculously, absurdly young! One forgets."

He took his hand from her chin and picked up her chiffon wrap, which had fallen to the floor when he had taken her into his arms.

"Come!" he said. "I will take you back to the *Hotel Meurice*."

His voice seemed hard and abrupt.

He walked to the door, opened it and Vada passed through it.

She stood indecisive and bewildered on the small landing outside as he locked the door and started down the stairs ahead of her.

She followed him, feeling that everything had gone wrong.

It was hard to understand why the ecstasy they had found together had been turned off like a light and now there seemed to be only darkness and a fog of indecision.

When they reached the street outside the tall building, Pierre saw in the distance a carriage drawn by one horse, moving slowly as if tired.

He gave a shrill whistle and the *cocher* turned round and drew his vehicle to a standstill.

"We are in luck!" Pierre said in what Vada thought was an almost indifferent tone.

They walked side by side briskly towards the carriage.

He did not take her arm as he had done before and, although he opened the door, he did not assist her to climb inside.

He told the *cocher* where to go and the horse started off again, clip-clopping over the cobblestones towards the bridge of *Notre Dame*.

Vada sat upright, her hands clasped together.

She was vividly conscious that Pierre was sitting in the corner of the carriage as far away from her, she thought, as he could.

He did not speak and, after they had gone a little distance, she said with what was a sob in her voice,

"Are you – angry with – me?"

"No."

"Then why are – you taking me – back?"

"You did not wish to stay any longer."

"I am s-sorry."

"Are you really sorry?"

Before she could answer, he said in another tone,

"No! That is an unfair question. You were right, quite right, Vada, to stop me."

"It was – silly of me to be – frightened."

"It was very sensible!" he contradicted her.

There was silence and then after a moment Vada said in a very small voice,

"Will you – ask me out – again?"

It seemed to her that there was a long pause before Pierre said,

"I am going away tomorrow. I have to go to the country to interview an artist for an article I am writing about him in *La Plume*. If you are still here when I return, I will give myself the pleasure of calling upon you."

Vada clutched her fingers together convulsively.

He was angry! He had not spoken to her in that formal tone the whole evening and now he was going away and she would not see him again.

"Please – "

She turned towards him impulsively.

" – please – I don't – understand what I have – done or why you are – cross with me."

Pierre was looking straight ahead and for a moment he did not turn to look at her.

Then, as she waited, her eyes on his face, which she could see quite clearly in the street lamps, he turned to her slowly.

He looked at her anxious, pleading little face and then put his arm around her and drew her against him.

It seemed to Vada as if she had stepped back into Heaven because he was no longer angry with her.

She hid her face against his shoulder and, because she

still did not understand what had happened, she said,

"I am sorry – so very very sorry – to have – spoilt the evening."

She felt his arm tighten a little as she went on,

"It was the most wonderful – the most perfect thing that has ever – happened to me in my whole life!"

"Do you really mean that?" Pierre asked.

"How can I – convince you? Now I know that I have never been – happy before."

He was silent before he said,

"Listen to me, Vada, I want you to promise me something. I want you to swear it by everything you hold sacred."

She raised her face.

"What is – it?" she asked in a whisper, afraid of the new solemnity in his voice.

"You must swear to me," he answered, "that you will never, under any circumstances, go alone to a man's apartments or his house at night, nor for that matter in the daytime."

"Was it very – wrong to come to – your studio?" Vada asked.

"Shall we say it was an indiscretion that must not be repeated, certainly not in Paris."

"W-why?"

She thought, as he did not answer immediately, that he was choosing his words with care.

Then he said,

"I frightened you a little and you might be very much more frightened with someone else, someone who would not have brought you home when you asked to go."

"You mean – that he might have gone on – kissing

me?"

"He might have done that and other things besides."

"What – other things?"

"That is something you need not know," he answered, "for the simple reason that you are giving me your promise. Give it to me, Vada."

"I promise you that I will – never go to a man's rooms – alone."

"Surely you should be chaperoned instead of being allowed to come to Paris with no one but a maid?" he asked.

She thought he sounded irritable.

"Miss Holtz should – have been with me," she explained. "It's – just that she has been – detained for a short while."

"But her mother allowed you two girls to leave New York with only a servant! It seems incredible!"

How could she explain, Vada wondered. Quickly, so that he would not pursue this line of thought, she said,

"I will keep my – promise, but I did want to – see your studio."

"Perhaps I will take you there when I come back," Pierre said, "but *not at night*."

He seemed to say the last words to himself.

Vada realised that they had now reached the *Rue de Rivoli* and in a few moments they would be at the hotel.

"Please – will you try to come back before I – leave Paris?" she asked.

"It depends."

"Upon – what?" Vada asked.

"The truthful answer is it depends on what I feel tomorrow morning," Pierre replied. "I think, Vada, tonight we have both been infected by some special magic. Perhaps in the morning we shall both feel very differently."

"I shall still feel it was the most – wonderful thing that has ever happened," Vada whispered.

Even as she spoke the carriage drew up outside the door of the *Hotel Meurice* and a porter hurried down the steps to open the door.

There was nothing Vada could do but alight.

She stood under the colonnade of the *Rue de Rivoli* and looked at Pierre.

"Will you come in – with me?" she asked.

She could not bear to say goodbye and could not bear to think that this might be the last time she would ever see him.

He seemed so aloof and in a way autocratic, despite the strangeness of his dress.

Yet he was the same man she had talked to at dinner and who had brought her an ecstasy that she had not believed existed when he had kissed her by the Seine.

"That is another thing you should not ask of any man who brings you home," he declared.

"It is – wrong?" Vada asked in a bewildered voice.

"Again, somewhat indiscreet,"

"But you are – different."

"I am glad you think so," he answered. "Perhaps one day you will realise how different from the other men you may meet."

He paused and took her hand in his.

"That is why I am going to say goodnight, Vada. Go to bed and dream of Verlaine's poetry and Wagner's music. I hope we shall meet again before you leave Paris."

Just for a moment his lips touched her hand.

Helplessly, knowing that there was nothing more she could do or say, Vada walked into the doorway of the hotel.

Inside she turned to look back, but Pierre was already climbing into the *voiture*.

She hoped that he might wave at her, but instead he must have sat back immediately in the seat and not looked to see if she was still watching him.

The horse and carriage disappeared from sight and, feeling bereft with a loneliness beyond anything she had ever known before, Vada went slowly up the stairs.

In her room she sat for a long time before she undressed, remembering the rapture of his kisses, the strange sensation she had felt when he had kissed her neck and her fear when he had begun to undo her gown.

Of course it had been wrong for her to allow him to do any of those things.

Yet it had not seemed wrong, but so completely and utterly right. More right than anything she had ever done in her life before.

'This is what I feel,' she told herself, 'and it is not what I ought to think. I am a Symbolist.'

She walked across the room and pulled back the curtains from the window.

She thought of the lights that she had seen from Pierre's studio, lights which had seemed like stars, and she knew that the memory of them would always be with her in her heart.

She felt a panic of fear that she might never see him again.

Yet when they had said goodbye, it was as if he was anxious to get away and was not really interested in meeting her again.

Then suddenly a terrible and horrifying thought came to her, supposing he had thought her cheap? Supposing he despised her because she had allowed him to kiss her?

Vada knew that no lady should have behaved in the way she had. But the question of position or rank had not seemed of any importance when she was with Pierre.

Everything they had done, everything they had said, had been so natural and when he had kissed her –

She drew a deep breath that came from the very depths of her being.

'I shall never forget,' she thought, 'not if I live to be a hundred, I shall never forget!'

*

The following morning Vada was waiting for Charity so that they could go together to Worth's shop to try on more gowns, which he had assured them would be ready by noon.

Vada had hoped that perhaps there would be some message from Pierre – just a line that he might have written after their evening together.

Then she told herself that, if there was to be a letter at all, it should come from her. She should thank him for giving her dinner.

'I will write to him,' she told herself.

She felt her spirits rise a little at the thought that even a letter would draw him a little closer to her.

Then she remembered that she did not know his address.

It seemed incredible that he had walked into her life only yesterday to fill it to the exclusion of all else. Yet she had no idea where he lived or what was the address of his studio where he had taken her last night.

And then she realised that she could write to him at the offices of *La Plume*.

Surely the address would be printed somewhere in their magazine if she could find a copy of one?

Then somehow the idea of writing to an office swept away the wish to communicate with him. Supposing a secretary or Léon Deschamps opened the letter in his absence?

'He has gone – and I may never see him again.'

It was a cry that had been echoed over and over again in her heart all night.

She had not been able to sleep, one moment quivering with ecstasy at the memory of Pierre's lips on hers, and the next moment tossing and turning in utter misery because she felt that he would not come back.

He had said that it all depended on what he felt this morning.

It was an incredible pain not to be able to know what he felt!

Charity had exclaimed at the dark lines under Vada's eyes when she had called her.

"Whatever time did you get back last night, Miss Vada?"

"I don't think it was very late," Vada answered vaguely.

Feeling a further explanation was necessary, she added,

"I did not sleep well."

"It's that foreign food you're so keen on," Charity said sharply. "It gives one indigestion. The stomach just can't

~108~

take it."

Vada did not answer and Charity rambled on,

"The sooner we get back to America and have some decent meals, not mucked about with all those rich sauces, the better! That's what I says!"

It was strange, Vada thought, but she could hardly remember now what she had eaten last night.

It had been delicious, the ambrosia of the Gods. But all she could remember vividly was Pierre's eyes looking into hers, Pierre talking, listening to what she had to say, making their small table in the corner of the restaurant seem a place of enchantment.

There was a knock at the door.

When Vada called "*entrez*", a pageboy entered the room.

"A gentleman to see you, Miss Sparling."

"A gentleman?"

Vada's heart gave a sudden leap.

Pierre had not forgotten her after all.

But, as she waited, a light in her eyes, the gentleman who came into the room was the Marquis de Guaita.

He was looking even smarter and more elegant than he had in Worth's shop.

"*Bonjour, mademoiselle*."

Vada dropped him a small curtsey.

She felt an almost ridiculous sense of disappointment that he was not Pierre.

"I have come" the Marquis said, "to enquire when Miss Holtz will arrive in Paris."

"I-I don't – know – exactly," Vada stuttered in reply.

"The inestimable Mr. Worth informed me who you were," the Marquis went on, "and, when I related to my mother that I had met you, she told me that she was an old friend of Mrs. Holtz's. She is therefore anxious to entertain Mademoiselle Emmeline as soon as she arrives in Paris."

"I will tell her of your kind invitation," Vada said formally.

"But you have no idea when she is expected?"

"Perhaps in a few days," Vada replied. "I am not sure."

The Marquis looked around the comfortable sitting room.

"May I sit down?"

"I am sorry," Vada said quickly. "I must seem very inhospitable. Please be seated, *monsieur*, and can I offer you some refreshment?"

"A glass of wine would be very acceptable," the Marquis answered.

Vada rang the bell.

Then reluctantly she sat on a sofa facing the Marquis. She hoped that he would not stay long. She wanted to get her fittings over at Worth's and go with Charity to see some of the sights of Paris.

Almost as if he read her thoughts the Marquis said,

"I gather this is your first visit to Paris, *mademoiselle*. I hope you have a competent guide to show you all the sights?"

"I hope to see them all," Vada answered.

"You don't mean to say that you and your maid are struggling around alone?"

"There is no alternative." Vada replied, "until Miss Holtz arrives."

"Then you must allow me to assist you," the Marquis said. "I know what inveterate sightseers Americans are and

I assure you that I am an extremely experienced Courier."

He smiled as he spoke and Vada realised that he was trying to be very pleasant.

But there was something about him that she did not like, she thought, and then she told herself that it was merely because she was comparing him with Pierre.

Pierre had left Paris and it was doubtful if he would return. In the meantime she would be very stupid if she refused to see more of this delectable city just because he was not with her.

"Which places do you suggest I visit, *monsieur*?" she asked.

"I was wondering if you would allow me to take you driving in the *Bois de Boulogne* this afternoon." he said, "and perhaps you would dine with me this evening?"

Vada waited.

She thought perhaps the Marquis would say that they would dine in the company of other friends, but he said no more and she answered hastily,

"It is very kind of you, *monsieur*, I am very anxious to see the *Bois de Boulogne*."

"But you have not answered my question about dinner." he said. "Perhaps I should add that no American would wish to leave Paris without seeing the *Moulin Rouge*,"

"*The Moulin Rouge*!"

Vada found herself echoing the words and there was a glint of excitement in her eyes that had not been there earlier.

"Would you really take me there?" she asked.

"Of course," he answered, "I am an *habitué* and I promise you that it is a sight you should not miss. There is nowhere else like it in the whole world."

"Then thank you very much!" Vada said. "I would be very grateful and, as you say, it is where every American tourist wishes to go."

"You have read about it in New York?"

"A great deal," Vada answered.

"About the Paris that is considered so naughty!" the Marquis remarked with a twist of his lips, "and yet it can be very attractive."

"I have found that out already," Vada smiled.

"You know they are calling this *La Belle Époque*." he said, "The Beautiful Time."

"And that is what I am quite sure it will be when its history comes to be written," Vada answered. "When I arrived at Cherbourg, I thought that I was stepping into a page of history."

"That is exactly what you are doing," the Marquis said, "and you and I, Miss Sparling, must be quite certain that we play our part in it."

He rose to his feet.

"If you will forgive me, I will not wait for the glass of wine. Paris hotels have not the quickness of New York."

"I quite understand," Vada said.

"But I will call for you at three o'clock," he said. "We will drive around the *Bois de Boulogne* and make our plans for this evening. I feel sure they will amuse you."

"I am sure they will," Vada answered, "and thank you very much."

She curtseyed, the Marquis bowed and he was gone before a waiter arrived to ask what was required.

*

'It is exciting,' Vada thought, as the Marquis drove her in his smart phaeton through the *Bois de Boulogne*.

Never had Vada seen such elegant victorias, coupés and landaus, such beautiful occupants, such fine horseflesh.

Everyone seemed to vie with everyone else to appear smarter, more original and even flamboyant.

It seemed impossible in view of the beautiful drives, the cascades, fountains and the profusion of flowers, that the *Bois de Boulogne* had ever been a real forest.

Now it was deliberately picturesque in the manner that Napoleon III had planned it.

Looking round Vada could understand that someone had once said,

"Apart from the earth and the trees everything is artificial in the Bois de Boulogne. All that is missing is a mechanical duck!"

But there was no need, Vada discovered, for mechanical birds or animals.

Le Jardin Zoologique d'Acclimatation was pointed out to her by the Marquis, who told her it that had been designed to breed and acclimatise foreign animal and vegetable species.

They also passed the hothouses, the Silkworm Rotunda, the great Aviary, the Poulerie and the Aquarium.

But it was difficult to have eyes for anything but those who were promenading round the lake gay with its gondolas, hoping that their jewels, their clothes, their horses and their coachmen would incite the envy of their friends.

Concentrating on driving his team, the Marquis did not say much, but when he did Vada thought that there was a flirtatious look in his eyes.

He also spoke to her in a slightly more familiar tone than he would have adopted had he thought her to be Emmeline Holtz.

But she was determined to make use of him to see Paris.

Nancy Sparling had told her to enjoy herself and to use her eyes. But she wanted also to make the most of the opportunities she might never have again.

She remembered her promise to Pierre and told herself that she would certainly not allow the Marquis to take her back to his apartment, should he suggest it, after they left the *Moulin Rouge*.

But it seemed to her, despite the glint in his eyes, that the Marquis was behaving most circumspectly.

She felt sure that if his mother was a friend of Mrs. Holtz he would not go out of his way to offend anyone in the Holtz's employment.

When the Marquis drove her back to the *Meurice*, she thanked him effusively for taking her to the *Bois de Boulogne*.

"I will call for you at seven o'clock, *mademoiselle*," he told her, "so that we can dine before we go to the *Moulin Rouge*."

Vada was just about to ask him a little nervously where he intended to take her when he answered the question for her.

"I thought you would like to dine at the *Grand Véfour*," he said. "It serves, in my opinion, the best food in Paris."

"I would like that," Vada said, "and thank you very much for suggesting it."

Tonight, she told herself as she dressed for dinner, there was no question of looking subdued or of not appearing out of place amongst a crowd of very poor poets.

At the same time she thought it would be a mistake, as the supposed companion of Emmeline Holtz, to appear overdressed.

She therefore chose, not one of her new gowns which she thought might make the Marquis suspicious, but one that she had bought in New York and which was far less elaborate than anything that came from the magic hands of the great Worth.

It was, however, very becoming, of forget-me-not blue. It was trimmed with yards of soft lace around the hem and the same lace edged the low *décolletage* and frothed over Vada's white arms.

Jewellery was, of course, out of the question, but she tied a little bow of ribbon of the same colour around her neck and a snood of the same velvet was worn like a halo at the back of her head.

Frenchwomen all wore hats in the evening, which to Vada looked strange and besides she had not yet found a milliner.

She made a note to ask Mr. Worth the following morning which would be the best shop to patronise.

Charity gave her a wrap of velvet the same colour as her dress.

As it was summer, it was trimmed not with fur but with swansdown and Vada hoped that the Marquis would not think it too opulent for someone in the position of a companion.

Equally she knew that unless he had thought that she was only an employee of the rich Miss Holtz and of no social consequence, he would not have asked her out alone. It would have been an insult.

When the Marquis called for her, he exclaimed,
"*Vous êtes ravissante!*"

It was impossible not to be pleased at such a compliment and Vada hoped it would take away the unbearable ache in her heart that had persisted all day.

She tried not to think about Pierre.

Her practical common sense told her that it was no use spoiling what was left of her visit to Paris just because she was missing a man she had only met the day before.

But he had crept into her life and, although she tried to tell herself that it was only imagination, he had altered her whole world.

She knew with an unmistakable conviction that when Pierre had kissed her he had awakened her to the love that she always dreamed was waiting for her somewhere.

"*L'amour toujours monte comme la flamme.*"

She could hear Verlaine saying the words.

Then, when Pierre had kissed her, a flame had flickered inside her to rise until she must acknowledge it and know that it was in fact love.

'I will not think about him – I will not!' she told herself.

Yet he was there! His face always in front of her eyes, his lips possessing hers!

"I must concentrate on the Marquis and the places he is taking me to,' she told herself as they entered the *Grand Véfour.*

It was smaller than she had expected. But she had read about the *Palais Royal* and how, when it had been the Palace of the famous Duc d'Orleans, he had overnight become the richest man in France because he had turned it into a place of enjoyment, of gambling houses and restaurants.

A place where, Vada gathered, all the prettiest women in Paris congregated for the delectation of the gentlemen.

Practically all that remained of the wild gaiety, the extravagance and the impropriety of the period was the *Grand Véfour*.

Its walls were still decorated with delicately beautiful *Directoire* frescoes under the Louis XVI ceiling, which had been there at the time of the Revolution.

There were comfortable red sofas all round the room and, as Vada looked round at the other diners, the Marquis said,

"It was here that Josephine dined with Napoleon Bonaparte at the beginning of their love affair!"

"Was it really?" Vada cried.

"And Fragonard, the painter of exquisitely beautiful women, died at the age of seventy-four after eating a maraschino ice here!"

Vada laughed.

"We must be careful."

But, when the food came, it was difficult not to eat to excess as Fragonard had done! It was so superlative it was beyond praise.

"Tell me about yourself," the Marquis said. "Are all young American women as unconventional as you?"

"What do you mean – unconventional?" Vada asked a little uncertainly.

"You have come to Paris apparently alone," the Marquis answered, "and for a beautiful woman that might be very dangerous."

Vada thought of Pierre's warning last night.

Then she put up her chin.

"I am American," she replied. "If we do

unconventional things, people excuse us because they think that we know no better!"

The Marquis laughed.

"That is a very evasive and very disarming reply," he said. "And now, tell me why you find Paris so attractive?"

"There is so much to see and so much to learn," Vada answered him.

"In what way?" he enquired.

"Across the Atlantic we really believe that all new thoughts, new ideas and new fashions come from Paris."

He laughed and started to talk to her about the new scientific inventions which, he claimed, were making France the envy of the world.

He seemed to know a great deal about science and he was also extremely well read.

And yet there was still something she did not like about him, she only wished she could understand what it was. No one could have been more flattering, no one more attentive.

When they drove off in the Marquis's closed carriage drawn by a pair of extremely impressive jet-black horses, Vada was half-afraid that he would try to be familiar.

But he made no attempt to touch her.

When they reached Montmartre, Vada leant forward excitedly to see *La Butte Sacrée*, which was not only a place of pleasure but the Sacred hill of St. Denis, the first Bishop of Paris.

They had passed through the *Pigalle* area, which, the Marquis remarked laconically, was famous for thieves, smugglers, tricksters, conjurers, pimps and singers, gypsies and prostitutes.

Then she stepped out into the flaring lights of gas jets

and electric signs to stare up entranced at the huge red sails of the windmill turning above her head.

The *Moulin Rouge* had opened its doors for the first time in 1889 and made the *Can-Can* world-famous.

After the Franco-Prussian War, Vada had read, the dance was popular amongst the working classes who called it *le Chahut*, a word that she translated as meaning 'din and rumbustiousness'.

Inside the *Moulin Rouge* she found a large hall with tables round the dance floor and an orchestra in the balcony.

The Marquis was bowed in with some ceremony and was escorted to a special table, which Vada learnt was specially reserved for him night after night.

Vada looked around her excitedly. The place was packed.

"Tell me, where do these people come from?" she asked the Marquis.

He laughed.

"Some may come from the smart Social districts of *Poissy, Neuilly* and the *Faubourg St. Honoré*," he replied, "to rub shoulders with the local costermongers, the artisans, shop girls and clerks."

He smiled at Vada and added,

"You will also find large numbers of your countrymen ogling *les demi-mondaines* and *les jolies poules*!"

Vada did not understand what he meant, but she did not like to show her ignorance.

Instead she looked at the orchestra, which was playing Offenbach's music while a very lively waltz was taking place on the dance floor.

People were pouring in and what with the noise of the

rather brassy band and the voices of those calling for drinks, it was almost impossible to make oneself heard.

No one appeared to take any notice of a variety of entertainments including a popular song and music hall acts.

Suddenly the band struck a resounding chord.

The music blared out and the dancing girls waving their full skirts took the centre of the floor.

Starting with a few elementary steps, they began to work themselves up to a frenzy, spinning round like tops and turning cartwheels and punctuating their gyrations with the famous high kick.

This, Vada realised, was the *Can-Can*!

It was a noisy stamping dance, quite unlike anything she had expected. There was something earthy and animal about it and the girls who performed it were not chosen for their looks.

Their dancing was crude, unabashed and finished up with the *grand écart* or splits, which meant they sat down violently on the floor, both legs stretched out absolutely horizontally.

Vada was not to know that many girls were injured for life by this exercise.

"Now," the Marquis said as they finished, "you will see *La Goulue*."

"Who is she?" Vada asked.

"Her real name is Louise Weber," he replied. "Her curious nickname literally means 'glutton'."

"Why is she called that?" Vada enquired.

"It comes from her habit of greedily sucking every last dreg from glasses," he replied.

"She is a dancer?" Vada asked in surprise.

"She has been a washer-girl, an artists' model and a dancer since she was in her teens," the Marquis answered.

As he spoke, amid shouts and whistles and cries from everyone present, *La Goulue* stepped onto the stage.

She was a heavy coarse blonde with a wilful, vicious, ruddy-hued baby-face.

Her mouth was wide, gluttonous and sensual and Vada could understand how she had acquired her nickname.

She started to dance slowly and, innocent though Vada was, she realised that what she was watching was something so immodest and in a way almost bestial that it made her acutely embarrassed.

Yards and yards of lace trimmed the inside of *La Goulue's* long skirt and when she kicked her legs high above her head, one after the other, it was easy to see two inches of bare flesh between her stockings and her frilly knickers.

What was more, the violence of her high kicks made her large white bosom appear to be in danger of escaping from her corsage. Never had Vada thought a woman could be so brazen or so outrageous in her behaviour, even on the stage.

She had heard of the *Can-Can,* but she had not been quite certain what she expected.

This, however, was disgusting – almost revolting!

Although it was almost beyond her comprehension, she somehow sensed that, without female grace, the fleshy woman outlined the lascivious meanderings of her coarse imagination with every twist and abrupt swirl of her hips.

Vada watched the performance with the colour rising in her cheeks until she felt that she could watch it no longer.

Then, as her eyelashes dropped and she looked away from what seemed to her a vulgarity beyond expression, she realised that the Marquis was watching her.

As if he sensed what she was feeling, he said quietly,

"Shall we go?"

"Yes – please."

Vada rose to her feet and they moved out across the crowded room where the patrons were calling, whistling and shouting for *La Goulue* to where the carriage was waiting outside.

They climbed in and, as they drove off, the Marquis enquired,

"You were shocked?"

"I was – surprised," Vada replied. "I did not – expect anything quite – like that."

His eyes were on her face as the candle lantern lit the inside of the carriage.

"You are very young."

Vada remembered that Pierre had said the same thing last night and she wondered why men kept referring to her age.

"Tell me something, *mademoiselle*," the Marquis asked. "Have you ever had a lover?"

For a moment Vada did not understand what he meant and then she was as shocked by his words as she had been by *La Goulue's* dance.

"No, of course not!" she answered indignantly, "and I think you have no – right to ask me – such a – question!"

"I was certain of it," the Marquis said in a low voice, "but I had to be sure."

Vada turned her face away from him to look out through the window as they went down the hill of

Montmartre.

"You are young, untouched and very beautiful," the Marquis said softly.

Vada wondered if he would consider her untouched if he knew that she had been kissed the night before.

Even to think fleetingly of Pierre made her ache for him.

How different her impressions of the *Moulin Rouge* were from the spiritual enlightening that she had received in the *Soleil d'Or*.

It was difficult to put it into words, but she knew that last night she had been enriched by all that she had experienced.

Tonight she had merely felt degraded.

Then she told herself that she had no right to complain.

She had wanted to go to the *Moulin Rouge* and, if she had been disappointed, that was her fault and she could not blame the Marquis who had been kind enough to take her there.

She turned towards him impulsively, only to find that he was still gazing at her with a strange expression in his eyes and somehow the words she had been about to say died away on her lips.

She did not know why, but she felt that there was something odd about him, something that she could not explain, but she only knew that it was there.

Then he suggested,

"Will you dine with me tomorrow night, Miss Sparling? I want you to meet a number of my friends. It will be an interesting party and I would so much like you to come."

Just for a moment Vada wanted to refuse and then she told herself that she would be very stupid if she did so.

The alternative to dining with the Marquis was to stay in the hotel listening to Charity complaining about France and wishing that she was back in New York.

Pierre would not have returned to Paris so soon and, even if he did so, he might not want to see her again.

The idea made her feel that there was an almost intolerable weight in her breasts.

Because she could not bear to think of Pierre, because she could not endure the thought that she might never see him again, she answered the Marquis quickly,

"It's very kind of you. I am delighted to accept your invitation to dinner, if you are sure that you have not had enough of me?"

"I am quite sure of that," the Marquis said. "Shall I call for you at seven o'clock?"

"I will be ready," Vada promised, "and thank you very much for tonight, I enjoyed the dinner enormously."

"But not the *Moulin Rouge*! Well, that is right! That is exactly how it should be!"

She looked at him a little surprised and he added,

"Young and innocent girls should not watch *La Goulue* without feeling nauseated."

"You make me sound very – stupid!" Vada sighed.

"Not stupid," he answered, "innocent and very beautiful. That is how you looked when you walked into Worth's Salon wearing that white gown."

Vada felt warmed by the admiration in his voice.

At least he thought that she was attractive, even if Pierre found it easy to go away and was not interested in seeing her again.

"You must tell me about your friends," she said, "and what interests them. It's always difficult to meet new people unless one has some idea of what one should talk about."

"They will have plenty to say to you," the Marquis said, "and I assure you that they will find you as unique as I do."

"Unique?" Vada questioned with a smile.

"You don't know," the Marquis replied, "how unusual, in fact unique, you are for Paris."

Chapter Six

In the morning there was a letter from Nancy Sparling. She wrote,

> *"I am afraid that my leg may take longer to heal than was expected, so it will be impossible for me to join you in Paris.*
>
> *What I suggest is that, as soon as you have finished your fittings or have enough gowns to set off for England, you should leave.*
>
> *I have been wondering if I did the right thing in letting you go there alone, but I am sure that you have been very sensible and have been able to look after yourself.*
>
> *Just send the Dowager Duchess a telegram telling her on which day and time you will be crossing the Channel and I am quite certain that you will find a Courier waiting for you at Dover to escort you to The Castle.*
>
> *I am very disappointed that I cannot show you Paris as I had intended to do – "*

There was a great deal more in the letter, but Vada could only concentrate on the sentences that told her she should leave for England.

She was well aware that, because Mr. Worth had done so much work on her gowns before she came to Paris, she already had quite a large enough wardrobe to take with her to England.

But how could she bear to leave?

She was not certain when Pierre would return or even

whether, when he did, he would wish to see her again.

Yet she knew that she could not bear to go away while there was still a hope that they might meet again.

As soon as they had finished breakfast, she and Charity set off for Worth's Salon, to find that even more gowns were ready than Vada had anticipated.

She had the feeling that they almost forced her into making the decision to leave Paris quite soon and she tried to find small things that should be altered, merely to delay the moment when they would be sent to the hotel.

They returned to the *Meurice* for luncheon and, when it was over, Charity asked,

"What do you wish to do this afternoon, Miss Vada?"

"I-I have not – made up my mind," Vada answered.

She rose to her feet and walked to the window.

There was so much she had wanted to see, so many sights that she had not yet seen, but unbelievably her enthusiasm had vanished!

She knew that Charity was anticipating that she would insist on visiting *Notre Dame* or going to the top of the Eiffel Tower.

Inexplicably, she had no wish now to do either, and yet, if she was honest with herself, the explanation was there.

It was because all the joy and excitement of Paris had gone with Pierre.

'I am being ridiculous!' Vada told herself. 'He was a man who came into my life unexpectedly and has left it just as quickly.'

But no amount of common sense could relieve the ache in her heart and the feeling that it was not worth bothering to see any more of Paris because it no longer

~127~

held any interest for her.

"Well, if you don't want me for the moment, Miss Vada," Charity said briskly, "I've some ironing to do and the chambermaid says I could use the ironing room down the passage."

"I will wait here until you have finished," Vada said.

"You're tired, that's what's wrong with you," Charity went on in her familiar scolding tones. "Out last night and the night before and all those fittings in the daytime. It's enough to exhaust anyone!"

Vada did not answer and she finished,

"If you take my advice, Miss Vada, you'll put your feet up on the sofa and read a nice book. You always used to enjoy doing that at home."

Charity went from the sitting room without waiting for a reply.

Vada stood at the window staring out at the trees in the *Tuileries* gardens, but seeing neither them nor the sunshine.

Instead she could see only Pierre's face and hear his voice when he had said,

"*Ma belle! Ma petite!*"

Why had she spoilt their evening together, she asked herself for the thousandth time.

Why had she been afraid when he had kissed her neck and her shoulders?

She could not explain to herself exactly what she had felt.

She had wanted him to go on kissing her. She wanted to feel the rapture and ecstasy that he had aroused in her and yet, for some reason she could not explain, it had frightened her.

'Why? Why was I so stupid?' she asked herself now.

She must have stood at the window for a long time and the depression that came from within her seemed to blind her to everything else.

There was a knock and the door opened behind her.

"A gentleman to see you, *m'selle*," a pageboy announced.

Vada turned round slowly and without much interest.

She supposed that it was the Marquis coming to make further arrangements about the dinner party.

Then the door closed behind her visitor and she saw who was standing there.

It was Pierre!

He wore the same green velvet coat and yet somehow he seemed larger, taller and more imposing.

As their eyes met, neither of them could move.

It seemed to Vada as if something magnetic passed between them, something vibrant and alive that had not been there before, something that made it impossible for her to speak, impossible even to move towards him.

"Pierre!"

Her voice sounded strange even to her own ears.

Her fair hair was silhouetted against the golden sunshine outside the window and for a moment she appeared to be encompassed in a cloud of glory before she broke the spell that had made her immobile.

She ran towards him.

"You have come back! You have come back!"

"Yes, I have come back," he answered in his deep voice, his eyes on her face.

She stopped just in front of him.

He made no attempt to touch her.

Her hands, which she had held out towards him, fell to her sides.

"I was afraid you would – forget about me," she said in a voice that was hardly above a whisper.

"I found it impossible to do so," he answered.

Her eyes searched his face enquiringly and he said,

"Put on your hat, I want to talk to you. We can go and sit in the *Tuileries* gardens."

Her eyes lit up and she flashed him a smile.

"I would like that."

She crossed the room to the door that led into her bedroom.

Hastily she pulled open the wardrobe and found a small straw hat trimmed with flowers and blue ribbons, which tied under her chin and matched the blue muslin gown that she was wearing.

She was glad that it was one of her prettiest dresses, but she had no time to think of herself.

Pierre was back and the whole world seemed suddenly a gloriously exciting, beautiful place again.

She hurried back to him.

He was standing in the sitting room almost where she had left him, and she thought that there was a serious expression on his face, but she was not certain.

He opened the door into the *entre-salle* for her and, as he did so, Vada said,

"Will you wait for a moment while I tell Charity I am going out, otherwise she will worry about me?"

"Of course," he answered.

"She is only down the passage."

They stepped into the corridor and Vada ran swiftly to the ironing room used by the chambermaids.

Charity was there pressing the gown that Vada had worn the evening before.

"I-I am just going out for a – walk with some friends," Vada said breathlessly.

"That'll be nice for you," Charity answered. "It'll stop you moping about. I don't know what's wrong with you, Miss Vada. I only hope you're not sickening for something!"

"I am all right!" Vada replied.

She turned and ran back down the corridor to where Pierre was waiting.

"Now we can go to the Gardens," she said.

Her eyes were shining like a child who had been promised a special treat.

"Come along then," he said and they went down the first two flights hand in hand before he released her.

They walked down the *Rue de Rivoli* and crossed the road to pass through the high iron gates that led into the *Tuileries* gardens.

It was the very picture of spring, Vada thought, with the purple lilacs, syringa scenting the air and the cherry blossom pink and white like Bouchet's cupids against the blue of the sky.

They seemed to have the Gardens to themselves and Pierre led the way to where, half-concealed by the low hanging branches of the trees, there was a seat.

They sat down and Vada turned towards him eagerly, her eyes seeking his.

"I was so – afraid you might not come back until I had – gone!"

"Are you thinking of leaving?"

She would not give him a direct answer.

Instead she said,

"I shall have to go – sometime."

"Yes, I suppose so," he answered, "but not at once and that is what I want to talk to you about."

Vada waited, suddenly tense. There was a note in his voice that she did not understand.

"We met each other really by chance," Pierre began, "and I think in that first moment we both knew that something we had not anticipated was taking place."

As he spoke, he deliberately turned his head aside so that he was no longer looking at her and she could only see him in profile.

"I am much older than you, Vada," he said. "At least eight years, and I have to think for both of us."

"Think about – what?" Vada asked, a little tremor in her voice.

"About ourselves," Pierre answered, "and whether what we felt the other night for each other was real or just an illusion. A very alluring illusion, but nevertheless an illusion!"

"I don't think I – understand."

Pierre smiled.

"It's very easy to be carried away by poetry, by music and, of course, by Paris!"

Vada was still and then she said in a lost little voice,

"You mean – when you – kissed me, it was not – important to you?"

"No, no, of course, I am not saying that."

He turned to her and took her hand in his.

"My darling, it was wonderful! Something so beautiful that I shall never forget it."

He saw the light come into her eyes and he continued,

"But because you are so young, I feel that I must give you time to think."

"About – what?"

"About yourself and about me."

He gave a little sigh.

"I am explaining myself very badly. What I am really trying to say is that I think things are moving too fast. We must take a little more time to get to know each other. There is so much for me to learn about you and for you to learn about me. If we allow ourselves to be swept away by the tide of our emotions, we might both regret it!"

Vada did not speak and he went on,

"You know so little about the world, while I know a great deal. You also know very little about love."

He released her hands to look out again across the Gardens.

"The reason I went away," he said quietly, "was that I thought I might feel very differently about you when I did not see you, but I had to come back."

"I am – glad about – that," Vada said a little breathlessly.

"But I am determined that we shall be sensible," Pierre went on. "We will see each other, talk together, and determine if what we feel for each other is really love or just a very good imitation."

Vada drew in her breath.

"But I thought – "

She stopped.

"Go on," Pierre encouraged.

"Perhaps I should not – say it," Vada answered. "You might think it – rude."

"I will risk it," he answered. "I want to hear what you

were about to say."

"It was – just that I think what you are – really saying," Vada said hesitatingly, "is that we must – be sensible, logical and – conventional. All the things I believed had nothing to do with – Symbolism."

Pierre gave a little laugh.

"You are right, my darling! Of course you are right! I am trying to think rather than to feel. At the same time, as always happens in life when something becomes very personal, we see everything in a very different light than when we are theorising."

"What do you – want us to – do?" Vada asked unhappily.

"At the moment," he answered looking at her again, "I only want to tell you that you are lovelier than I remembered, more entrancing than I believed it possible for any woman to be."

"Do you – mean that?"

"Now I am explaining what I feel," he answered with a little smile.

He took her hand in his again, holding it in both of his.

"We have to be sensible, *ma petite*," he said. "I know nothing about you, except that you are utterly adorable, and you know nothing about me except that I love you!"

Vada's eyes seemed to hold all the sunshine in the garden and her fingers tightened on his.

"Do you – really love – me?"

"I tried to tell myself it's an illusion," he answered, "but I failed."

"And I love you!" she said. "I love you – so much that it has been an agony I have never before known to think –

that I might never see you again."

"Oh, sweet darling!"

Pierre's voice was unsteady.

Then, turning her hand upwards, he kissed the palm, his lips lingering on the softness of her skin.

Vada felt a thrill run through her and she knew once again that he had awakened in her the flame that she had felt as they kissed beside the Seine.

Then he released her hand to put it firmly down in the lap of her dress.

"I love you, at the same time, Symbolism or no Symbolism, I am going to be sensible!" he said. "I have the feeling that you have met very few men in your life."

"N-not – many."

"Is your father alive?"

"No."

"Then if he was alive," Pierre said, "he would say, as I am saying, that you must not rush into anything knowing so little about men and life. Let's just enjoy ourselves. We will see Paris together. We will talk and laugh and for the moment not worry about the future. Do you agree?"

"I will agree to – anything as long as I can be with – you," Vada answered.

"We will be friends," Pierre went on, "friends who exchange ideas and don't make too many demands upon each other."

"I would – like to be your – friend."

"Then we are in agreement," Pierre smiled. "Where shall I take you for dinner tonight?"

"Anywhere," Vada answered and then gave a little cry.

"What's the matter?" Pierre enquired.

"It's just that I promised to dine with a party. I would

~135~

not have accepted – but I had no idea that you would come back so soon."

"Who are you dining with?" Pierre enquired.

"The Marquis de Guaita."

Pierre raised his eyebrows and Vada added,

"He called yesterday to find out when Emmeline Holtz was arriving. His mother is apparently a friend of Mrs. Holtz's."

"And, as Miss Holtz was not there, he took you out instead?" Pierre enquired.

"He – took me to the – *Moulin Rouge*," Vada told him a little uncertainly.

"Alone?"

The question was sharp.

"Y-yes," Vada stammered, "but he was – kind when I was – shocked."

"You were shocked?"

"Yes. It was so horrible! That woman who danced was disgusting! Degrading! I did not expect it – to be like that."

Pierre did not speak and she carried on,

"The – Marquis took me away a-and he seemed to – understand."

"He had no right to take you there alone."

"He behaved very – correctly except – "

Vada paused.

"Except what?" Pierre asked.

She thought unhappily that he was angry.

"He asked me a – question he had – no right to ask me."

"What was that?"

"He asked me – if I had a – l-lover!"

Vada blushed as she spoke. It was difficult to say the

~136~

word.

"How dare he insult you in such a manner?" Pierre exclaimed almost savagely.

"I-I don't think – that he meant – to be insulting," Vada went on, "because then he said that I was – young, innocent and – u-untouched."

Vada's voice trembled a little on the last word.

She was thinking of how Pierre had kissed her.

"I suppose he meant no harm," Pierre said grudgingly. "After all, he is a great friend of Joseph and together they have started the Kabbalistic Order of the Rosy Cross."

"What is that?" Vada asked.

"Péladan and Guaita claim it to be a revival of a Medieval Rosicrucian Sect. They have set up an entire religion and wear strange archaic costumes. Péladan has appointed himself Grand Master, besides designing his own Coat of Arms and appointing Archons and Grand Priors in the Order."

Pierre laughed.

"It all seems to be a lot of play-acting. Equally Péladan, who is very talented, has been writing plays inspired by Wagner and his own Babylonian obsessions. These were produced and have evoked a lot of artistic attention."

"It sounds very interesting," Vada said. "I wish I had known this last night."

"Péladan then became the impresario of Art Exhibitions which were most successful. The first Rosy Cross Exhibition was held last year and opened after a preliminary Mass had been said in *Notre Dame*."

"Did many people attend?" Vada enquired.

"According to *Figaro* it drew as many as eleven

thousand visitors. The Ambassadors of Sweden and America came and Péladan presided wearing a black doublet with lace cuffs and a ruff!"

Vada laughed.

"It sounds fascinating!"

"I was naturally interested," Pierre continued, "because Péladan is a great admirer of the painters favoured by the Symbolists and it was a chance for some of our struggling young men to get their pictures noticed."

"I would so much like to meet Mr. Péladan," Vada said.

"You must ask the Marquis to arrange it or perhaps he might even be at your dinner party tonight."

Vada was silent and then she said,

"Must I – go now that you have come back?"

"If you have promised to do so, I think that you should keep your promise," Pierre replied.

"I would so much rather be – with you."

"And I would have liked you to dine with me, but there is always tomorrow."

"Yes, I know," Vada said a little doubtfully, "but it seems a waste of one of my evenings in Paris."

Pierre smiled.

"If I ask you to have luncheon with me tomorrow, will that make it seem better?"

"Much – much better!" Vada smiled, "and can I dine – with you tomorrow night?"

"If I don't have a better engagement!" he answered and then, seeing the hurt in her eyes, added quickly,

"I am only teasing you and once again trying to be sensible. I would much rather you behaved like a Symbolist."

"If you look at me – like that," he said very quietly, "I shall find it difficult to remember I am anything else."

His eyes were on her lips and almost instinctively, without thinking, she moved a little nearer to him.

With an obvious effort he rose to his feet.

"Come and look at the Gardens," he suggested abruptly.

As the afternoon passed, they talked on every subject imaginable in a mixture of French and English.

Sometimes it seemed as if Pierre found it impossible to express what he wished to say except in French.

At other times Vada thought that when he spoke in English his words had a deep sincerity.

"When are you going to show me some Symbolist paintings?" she asked.

"I want you to see Gustave Moreau's works," Pierre answered. "He once said, '*one must only love, dream a little and refuse to be satisfied*'."

"Is that what you do?" Vada asked.

"I did until – " Pierre answered slowly with his eyes on her face. "I found something completely and absolutely satisfying."

Then quickly, as if he had said too much, he began to talk about Moreau's pictures, describing the mystic visionary composition of them.

Vada felt as if he kept pulling himself away from her and from their becoming too close to each other, not physically but mentally.

Once during the afternoon she exclaimed,

"I am happy – so very very happy!"

"To be in Paris?" Pierre asked.

"To be with – *you*."

There was a sudden silence between them and Vada went on,

"Today before you arrived – I found I no longer had any interest in seeing anything – or in doing any of the things I had planned."

"And now?"

"Everything has come alive! I can feel – the earth pulsating, the flowers and shrubs growing, the world breathing and I am a part of it – because you are – there."

Pierre turned his face away and said in a hoarse voice,

"If you talk to me like that, I shall forget that I am trying to be your friend."

"Can friends not – be wildly happy – because they are – together?"

"*Ma belle*! *Ma petite*! What am I to do about you?"

It seemed to Vada that there was an unexpected pain in Pierre's voice.

Then, as they looked into each other's eyes, the Gardens disappeared. There was only the sunshine, golden, blinding, compelling, in a world where there was no one else but themselves.

'I love – you!' Vada wanted to say, but she did not dare.

It was love that made her heart beat suffocatingly in her throat. Love that was a flame rising and burning in her breasts.

There was no need for Pierre to touch or kiss her, she vibrated to him like a musical instrument to a Master's touch.

There was so much to look at and so much to talk about that when finally Pierre took Vada back to the hotel there was only a short time left for her to change into her evening gown.

"I wondered what'd happened to you," Charity said, "but I guessed you'd be sight-seeing."

Vada did not disillusion her.

She felt as if the time that she had spent with Pierre in the *Tuileries* gardens was like being on an enchanted island.

It was difficult now to remember all they had talked about. She had felt that there was so much for her to learn, so much she wanted to know and that every moment she was with him she grew wiser as well as happier.

'*I love him*! I love him!' she told herself.

As she changed, she knew that as far as she was concerned it was an absurd waste of time to be going out with the Marquis or anyone else in the whole world when she might be with Pierre.

Yet she was feminine enough to remember that the Marquis had admired her in the white dress in which he had first seen her at Worth's.

Although she would not wear one of the magnificent exquisite gowns designed by 'the Master', which were now hanging in her wardrobe, she chose a white dress that had come from America.

It made her look very young and, as the Marquis had said, very innocent.

When she walked downstairs to find the Marquis waiting for her in the vestibule, she might have stepped straight out from Charles Gibson's easel.

It seemed to her that his dark eyes scrutinised her searchingly as she descended the last stair to hold out her gloved hand to him with a faint smile.

"My friends are looking forward eagerly to meeting you, Miss Sparling," he said courteously, "and I have counted the hours until this evening."

The words sounded smooth and all too fulsome, Vada thought, and she knew that had Pierre said them they would have contained a special meaning that would have made her thrill.

The Marquis's comfortable carriage was waiting outside and they drove through the *Place de la Concorde* and up the *Champs Élysées*.

"Where are we going?" Vada asked.

"To the house of the Comte de Rochegude," he answered. "He is a friend of mine and has a larger dining room than I have in my comparatively small flat."

"It is a big party, then?"

"We shall be thirty," he answered.

Vada could not help hoping that she would not be overwhelmed by the elegance and *chic* of the other ladies present.

However, to her surprise she found the party predominantly male.

It was true that there were four other women present, but they were middle-aged and, while one of them was exotically gowned, the others, despite their high-sounding titles, looked dull and unfashionable.

The men were of all ages and they vied with each other in paying Vada extravagant compliments.

She could not help thinking with a touch of amusement that if Pierre really wished her to meet other men, his wish was certainly being granted this evening.

The Comte de Rochegude's house was large and impressive.

At the same time there was an atmosphere, Vada thought, of deep gloom about it.

The rooms seemed too high, the tapestries were sombre against the panelled walls and the lights appeared to be sparse and low after the brilliance of the hotel.

Everyone else had assembled before the arrival of Vada and the Marquis.

Almost immediately they left the Salon where the Comte received them to make their way along corridors that led to the back of the house where the dining room was situated.

It was not a conventional dining room, Vada thought, but more like a Baronial Hall draped with blood-red curtains.

The chairs had strange crests and Coats of Arms on them and the long table was decorated with an amazing display of gold and silver goblets of every shape and size.

The servants who waited on them were dressed in Medieval costume and served the food on plates of gold.

Vada gazed around the room in an attempt to take in every detail so that she could relate it to Pierre and ask him to explain their meaning.

She felt sure that the furnishings and the goblets on the table were connected with the Order of the Rosy Cross.

She did not like to ask the Marquis outright in case he would feel it embarrassing to talk about religion at such a secular moment as a dinner party.

It was certainly a dinner that Vada was unlikely to forget.

Never had she seen such a varied array of exotic dishes or so many different wines.

There was a wine for every course and the courses themselves all seemed to be comprised of unusual ingredients. Some were delicious, but others she pushed to the side of her place and hoped that no one would notice that she was not eating them.

The Marquis, who was sitting next to her, kept pressing her to try the wines and, as she did not like to keep refusing, she took a tiny sip of each.

Fortunately the goblets out of which they drank, some of which were set with precious stones, did not show, as a glass would have done, how little wine she consumed.

While Vada was abstemious, it was obvious that the other guests were eating and drinking in a manner that made her feel that they must have been hungry and thirsty when they arrived.

What surprised her was that the party appeared to have little to say.

There was none of the sparkling witty conversation that she had expected.

Finally the long drawn out meal began to come to an end.

The servants extinguished all the candles in the room with the exception of those on the table.

The faces of the people seated round the table suddenly assumed a macabre appearance.

As Vada looked at them, the Marquis said,

"Let us now drink a toast to our guest of honour, the lovely, young, innocent and pure Miss Nancy Sparling."

He rose to his feet and raised his glass and the rest of the company followed suit, although a little unsteadily.

Vada knew that she must remain seated.

Feeling embarrassed at the attention she was receiving, the colour rose in her cheeks.

She managed, however, to smile and bow her head as they raised their goblets and drained them.

"Now you must drink to us," the Marquis said.

As he spoke, he handed Vada a goblet which she thought resembled a chalice. It was gold and set with deep red rubies that flickered like fire in the light of the candles.

She took it from the Marquis's hands a little uncertainly.

There was an expression in his eyes that she did not understand and she could find no explanation for.

It was a look of excitement, she thought, almost of triumph!

Then she told herself that she was being imaginative and it was only a trick of the candlelight.

The guests were all watching and waiting, their heads down the long table all turned in her direction.

Vada did not rise because she felt shy.

"Drink it all!" the Marquis commanded. "Do you understand? You must drink it all!"

Vada looked down into the goblet.

There seemed to be a great deal of dark red wine in it and she knew that she did not wish to drink so much.

She was used only to an occasional glass of champagne or white wine at festivals, birthdays or very special occasions.

She wondered frantically how she could refuse and then knew that whatever she said would seem rude.

"I drink your health and thank you for drinking mine," she said in a shy voice and lifted the goblet to her lips.

The wine tasted horrible!

Not only was she afraid of drinking too much, but also she knew that it was so unpleasant she might be sick!

"Drink it! Drink it all!" the Marquis insisted.

Quite suddenly Vada remembered a trick she had

played on her nurse when she had been forced to drink some unpalatable medicine.

Making as if to raise the goblet to her lips again, she suddenly pointed with her left hand to the wall opposite.

"Look! Look!" she cried.

As she had anticipated, everyone turned in the direction of her finger and she took the chance to tilt the goblet sideways and the wine was spilled to the floor.

"What did you see? What was it?" the Marquis asked.

"I thought I saw a – bird." Vada replied, "but perhaps I was mistaken, it must have been just the candlelight casting shadows on the walls."

The Marquis turned to look at her as she gave her explanation, as did everyone else at the table.

Feeling embarrassed at her deception, Vada lifted the goblet and drained the last few drops of wine.

She put the goblet down on the table.

As she did so, she was aware of a silence in the room.

Everyone at the table was still watching her.

They were not speaking. Just watching and waiting.

Then it seemed to Vada that she saw nothing but their eyes, eyes getting larger and larger and coming nearer and nearer.

She tried to cry out, tried to rise from her seat, but even as she did so she knew that it was too late!

A thick suffocating darkness came up from the floor to cover her.

*

Pierre walked into the *Soleil d'Or* expecting to find Léon Deschamps there.

He wanted to talk to him about various matters, but, although there were a number of people present, Deschamps had not yet arrived.

Pierre spoke to several of his friends as he moved to his usual table near the stage.

Drawing some papers from his pocket, he spread them out in front of him and began to correct an article that was to be included in the next edition of *La Plume*.

He was not particularly impressed with the way that it had been written and one of the items he wished to discuss with Deschamps was how they could improve the quality of the articles that were appearing in *La Plume*.

Pierre felt the magazine had become less inspired and more banal than had been the case the previous year.

The room became more crowded, although there was never as large an attendance early in the week as there was at the end.

Someone went to the piano to play a rather indifferent composition, but, if there were poets present, they were disinclined to proclaim their poetry, at any rate not until later in the evening.

Pierre finished his writing and had ordered himself a second drink, when he saw Joseph Péladan walking towards him.

He moved towards Pierre looking, as usual, fantastic.

He was wearing over a strangely-fashioned black suit an enormous gold chain, attached to which was a pendant adorned with mystic symbols, Rosy Crosses and winged Assyrian bulls.

"Joseph! This is a pleasant surprise!" Pierre exclaimed.

"I thought I should find either you or Deschamps here," Joseph Péladan replied, "and I have with me Léo

Taxil."

"We have not met for some time," Pierre said.

He knew Léo Taxil, a resourceful and unscrupulous journalist, whose real name was Gabriel-Antoine Jogard-Pages and, who had become one of the best-known exposers of occultism in France.

He had a genius for spreading the most preposterous stories and worked on the principle that the bigger the lie the more readily people will swallow it.

Pierre had never liked the man, but he had to admit that he had managed to convince a great number of people, including Church Officials both in France and abroad, that Black Magic and Freemasonry were inseparable.

He had also published a great number of books which, it was said, had influenced the Pope to issue an Encyclical against the Freemasons.

The previous year Taxil had published a highly successful series of pseudo-revelations and his last book was entitled *Are There Women in Freemasonry?*

As they sat down at the table, Pierre was quite convinced that, if Taxil was enlisting the help of Joseph Péladan, he had some new scheme in mind, undoubtedly lucrative for himself.

"What can I do for you?" Pierre said, after they had ordered wine. "We are, Joseph, of course honoured that you should come to the *Soleil d'Or* again after so long an absence."

"You know quite well that I have not forgotten the Symbolists," Joseph Péladan said, "but I have had a great many other things to occupy my mind recently."

"I know that," Pierre said with a slight smile.

He waited and after a moment Joseph Péladan went

on,

"Léo has convinced me that there are even more things for me to do. He tells me that the secret orgies that are taking place in Masonic Lodges have reached such proportions that only someone of my authority and standing can combat their evil."

"Is Black Magic and Devil Worship more rife than usual?" Pierre asked with a faint touch of sarcasm in his voice.

"Much more!" Léo Taxil replied. "The worship of Lucifer is beginning to take a hold over the whole of France. There are child sacrifices, conjuration of devils and blasphemous Masonic rites being enacted in a way that sooner or later will destroy the whole country!"

Pierre knew that Léo Taxil always exaggerated. At the same time there was undoubtedly a certain amount of truth in what he said.

Many Church Authorities and scholars were, as Pierre knew, worried by the vogue of the supernatural at a time when anti-clericalism was widespread in France.

Magic and the occult appealed to many young men of artistic inclinations and it was true that the craze for it had acquired for Paris a sinister reputation as the centre for Black Magic.

The Paris press regularly published stories of sorcery and mysterious cults and one journalist had described in a newspaper article how he had been taken blindfolded to a house in Paris where he witnessed a Satanic ritual followed by an orgy.

"How do you want me to help you?" Pierre asked.

"Léo is bringing out a periodical publication to be called *The Devil and the Nineteenth Century* in which the worst of these abuses are to be exposed." Joseph Péladan said. "And we want the support of *La Plume* and of all well-known publications."

Pierre smiled to himself.

He might have guessed that Taxil would do everything in his power to make his periodical a bestseller and, if he could obtain free publicity in other periodicals, it would obviously be a tremendous advantage.

"I will talk it over with Léon," Pierre said, playing for time. "In the meantime, if we could see an advance copy, it would naturally make things easier for us."

"You shall have one tomorrow," Léo Taxil said eagerly. "I would have brought it with me tonight, but it is still on the printing press."

"You have a great deal of new material, I suppose?" Pierre suggested. "After all you have already covered the subject pretty thoroughly in your books."

"I shall tell you of things you have never even dreamt of," Taxil said. "For instance there are experiments now taking place to draw the soul or spirit from the body and replace it with that of an elemental."

"Is that possible?" Pierre asked cynically.

Taxil shrugged his shoulders.

"It is certainly a new departure and something that involves drugs, Black Mass and the invocation of Satan."

He spoke with a kind of relish that Pierre found unpleasant.

To change the subject he said to Joseph Péladan,

"I was talking about you today and about the Order of the Rosy Cross."

Péladan, as he had expected, asked to whom.

"To an American who is dining tonight with your

~150~

friend Stanislas de Guaita."

"He is no friend of mine," Joseph Péladan said sharply.

"No friend of yours?" Pierre ejaculated in surprise. "Since when?"

"Guaita and I quarrelled some months ago," Péladan answered. "I don't approve of his behaviour or that of his friends."

"What do they do?" Pierre enquired.

Before Péladan could reply, Léo Taxil broke in with,

"They are studying the secrets of alchemy, the occult sciences and the conjuring up of spirits. Their objective at the moment is, as I have just told you, the transplantation of an elemental into the human body, having withdrawn its soul."

Pierre was very still.

"Are you telling me," he asked at length in a strange voice, "that Guaita has become a Satanist?"

"But, of course. That is why we quarrelled," Péladan answered.

"He will not succeed in his last ambition," Léo Taxil broke in. "Transplantation of souls can take place only when the victim is a virgin who is also pure and innocent."

He laughed unpleasantly as he added,

"Where do you think Guaita is going to find a girl like that in Paris?"

Pierre rose to his feet.

"Tell me," he said to Léo Taxil in a voice that was hoarse, "where do these orgies take place?"

"The Black Mass must be said in a consecrated Chapel," Léo Taxil answered.

"I know that!" Pierre said impatiently, "but where?

Tell me where?"

"What's the matter, Pierre?" Joseph Péladan asked.

Pierre put his hand on Taxil's shoulder.

"The address," he said in a voice of command.

"The de Rochegude house in the *Avenue du Bois* off the *Champs Élysées*."

Pierre turned and walked away down the room.

As he reached the door, he saw sitting at a table a number of young anarchists, one of whom he knew quite well.

He stopped.

"Jacques, have you a pistol with you?" he asked.

"But, of course!" Jacques replied.

"Then come with me, I need you."

*

There was a strange chanting, the voices deep and somehow guttural.

They impinged on Vada's consciousness, dragging her up through layers of darkness, so that, although she longed to sleep, she was forced to move towards the light at the end of a long tunnel.

The voices grew louder and louder.

She opened her eyes.

She could not understand, could not realise what was happening.

There were voices chanting all around her, men's voices deep and resonant. Although she could not understand the words, something in their tone made her shrink within herself so that she was afraid.

There were lights of candles and the sickly aroma of

incense.

Then she looked up and would have screamed.

Above her, towering towards the ceiling, was a crucifix and it was upside down.

Attached to it immediately over her was a huge bat, its wings outstretched. She could see its beady eyes, its pointed nose and the hooks on the end of its black wings.

Terror, like a hidden snake, seemed to uncoil itself inside her, but she could not scream.

She could not move her mouth!

Then she realised that she had no feeling in the whole of her body.

She closed her eyes in sheer horror!

It could not be true! She must be dreaming! It was a nightmare, so terrifying that she must somehow break it and wake!

She wanted to move, but she could not do so.

Tentatively, afraid with a fear that shot through her mind like a sharp sword, she opened her eyes a little.

What she feared was true.

She was naked!

She could see her breasts and she realised that she was lying stretched out at the foot of the upturned crucifix.

The voices were increasing in volume. Louder and louder.

They intoned what Vada vaguely thought were prayers, and yet they were like no prayers she had ever heard, except that they were in Latin.

She recognised several names.

Nisroch, the God of hatred. Moloch, the fatalist that devours children and Adramelech, the God of murder.

Now the voices cried out in French,

"Beelzebub, Adramelech, Lucifer, come to us! Master of Darkness we implore thee! Satan, we are thy slaves! Come! Come! Illuminate us with thy presence!"

They began another prayer in Latin, saying the words backwards.

At last Vada understood.

She was taking part in a Black Mass!

Catherine de Medici had used Black Magic in an attempt to hold the love of her husband whom she believed was spellbound by Diane de Poitiers.

There had been Papal denunciations against those who dabbled in the occult and especially in Black Magic.

Vada closed her eyes again.

It could not be true! Something strange must have happened to her mind that she should imagine such obscenities.

But she knew it was true, knew it while she lay there unable to move, unable to scream.

She tried to remember what happened after the Black Mass had been said.

Mercifully her information on this matter was not explicit.

All she knew was that she felt humiliated and degraded, lying naked and paralysed.

She realised that it was the drugged wine they had given her that had made her inanimate and her brain had returned to consciousness only because she had drunk so little of it.

Suddenly the enormity of the evil taking place made her feel that she was not only in physical but spiritual danger.

Physically they might kill her!

She knew that human sacrifices were made by those who worshipped the Devil, although vaguely she thought that the victim was usually a child or an animal.

There were other things that could be done to a woman, but she was not certain what they were.

She saw arms upstretched towards the bat hanging above her, arms encased in silken robes, embroidered with Kabbalistic symbols.

Vaguely she thought that they belonged to the Marquis, but she was not certain as she could not turn her eyes far enough to see.

Anyway, she was afraid to look at him.

She remembered the eyes of those at the dinner table who had stared at her, watching, waiting for her to drink the drugged wine, and she felt that she must die before they touched her.

The prayers went on and now she could catch a word here and there that she understood and she knew that they were once again calling down Satan in their midst and invoking devils.

"Belial in eternal revolt and anarchy – Ashtaroth, Nehamah, Astarte in debauchery."

It was then that Vada began to pray.

Because she was so frightened, she could only remember the prayers she had said as a child,

'Gentle Jesus, meek and mild, look upon this little child.

Suffer me to come to Thee that I may hide myself in Thee.'

In her fear she repeated the prayer over and over again,

'Gentle Jesus – gentle Jesus–'

Somehow the very repetition of the words in her mind seemed to take away a little of the horror encroaching upon her and coming, she felt, menacingly nearer and nearer.

She wondered somewhere at the back of her mind if Satan really appeared to those who called for him.

Then she told herself that they were mad!

But if he did come, God would protect her! She belonged to God, not to the Devil.

'Help me! Help me, God!' she tried to say and thought of Pierre.

He had told her to attend the party.

Perhaps God would make him realise that he had made a mistake and he would save her! Save her from this terrible encroachment of evil.

She felt that at any moment the men might touch her and she would feel their hands on her naked body.

Once again she tried to scream and found that her lips, like the rest of her body, were paralysed.

'*Gentle Jesus! Gentle Jesus!* Oh – Pierre! – *Pierre!*'

She wanted to cry out his name aloud.

She felt if she could do so he might hear her.

It was then that she saw the hands in their Kabbalistic robes held over her once again.

This time they were turned downwards.

She knew then they were using hypnosis or mesmeric powers over her body.

They were going to touch her!

Because she was so afraid she shut her eyes.

'Pierre – Pierre – '

She tried to cry out once more and, as she did so, she heard a crash.

"*Stop this blasphemy!*"

It was a voice loud with an authority that seemed to echo round the room and then there was a sudden silence.

The chanting stopped.

The hands hovering over Vada vanished.

There was the screaming of voices almost like the snarl of animals.

"Turn him out! Turn him out! He has no right!"

Then Pierre's voice rang out strong with authority, the voice of an avenging angel!

"If any man attempts to stop me, my friend here will shoot him!"

Chapter Seven

It was immediately obvious to Pierre that he was in a Satanic Temple.

On one curtain behind the altar there was embroidered the huge figure of a rearing goat and on the other the figure of a woman with seven breasts and a serpent's tail.

The Satanists fell back in front of him as he walked up the Chapel aisle and only the Marquis standing at the altar steps held his ground.

Jacques, with a pistol in his hand, walked behind Pierre looking from side to side and almost instinctively those present turned their eyes from his.

At the same time those who were not directly in Pierre's path were still murmuring against him.

The sound, animal and angry, seemed to grow in intensity until the moment when he confronted the Marquis.

Behind the Marquis was a Priest.

The altar was draped in gold with Vada's naked body lying on lace-edged linen.

Above her the huge upturned crucifix with the dark body of the bat with its wings outspread was an emblem of evil.

There were innumerable black candles and the smell of incense was almost sickening in its pervasiveness, containing as Pierre knew, erotic drugs.

But if his guests were afraid, the Marquis was not.

His eyes met Pierre's defiantly, the pupils dilated and black from the hashish he had taken.

"Go from here. Go! Do not interrupt us!" he commanded in a resonant voice that seemed to ring out in the Chapel. "This is the Temple of Lucifer the Mighty One and you have no power against him."

His words brought courage to his adherents and they moved forward angrily, as if they would attack Pierre and hurl him from the Chapel.

They were checked only by the sight of Jacques who, with his back to the altar faced them, his pistol pointing first at those on the right and then at those on the left.

In that second's pause Pierre knocked the Marquis down.

He caught him a hard uppercut on the chin and punched him with his left hand in the body.

The Marquis collapsed to the ground. The embroidered robes he was wearing fell open and he was naked!

It was then Pierre realised that everyone else present was naked save for their long robes made of expensive luxurious materials with embroidered cowls.

The Marquis gave a cry as he fell and there was blood oozing from the corner of his mouth.

Either his courage deserted him or the drug bemused his senses, but he made no attempt to rise again.

Pierre glanced down at Vada and, turning to the Priest who had backed against the altar as if for support, he seized his vestment off his shoulders and covered her with it.

Naked, the man shrank away into the shadows beyond the candles.

Gently Pierre raised Vada in his arms.

"Walk behind me and prevent them following," he said in a low voice to Jacques.

Without hurrying he carried Vada's draped body down the aisle of the Chapel and out through the door by which he and Jacques had entered.

Jacques followed him.

He looked back at the stricken Satanists who, with their leader prostrate on the ground and the Priest out of sight, were making no further effort to prevent Vada being taken from their midst.

Jacques followed Pierre through the open door and slammed it behind them.

"Lock it!" Pierre said. "It will give them time to come to their senses, if they have any!"

There was no key in the lock, but there were bolts on the door that obviously divided the Chapel from the main house and these Jacques shot into position.

Then he followed Pierre down a short corridor, which led to the Banqueting Room.

They had in fact entered the Count's house by one of the windows of the room where Vada had dined.

Pierre had thought that there would be servants in the front part of the house who would have been instructed to prevent anyone from disturbing their Master and his guests.

He and Jacques had therefore climbed into the garden encircling the house and found, as they had expected, that the Chapel had been built at the back.

It had stained glass Gothic windows by which it would have been impossible to enter.

But the Banqueting Room was different. It had long casements and one of them was open behind the red curtains that decorated the room.

It had been easy for them to slip inside.

The servants had obviously not entered the room after the guests had moved to the Chapel and the table was as they had left it with its profusion of goblets.

Jacques stared in astonishment.

There was no time for Pierre to explain to him that Satanists did the exact opposite to everything done by the Christians.

Because the Christians fasted before Mass, the Satanists dined first, eating and drinking to excess because it was a gesture of defiance of all that was Holy.

Once inside the house Pierre had hurried in the direction of the Chapel, the urgency of his fear for Vada making him move so swiftly that it was difficult for Jacques to keep up with him.

Because of what Léo Taxil had said, he was really afraid that she would be actually violated in some Satanic orgy.

These often left the female victim, over whom they said Mass, half-dead from the lustful abuse to which she was subjected afterwards.

And he was well aware of the terror that the Black Mass could inspire in those who must unwillingly take part in it.

He could only pray that Vada would be rendered unconscious before the start of the ceremony so that she would not be aware of what was happening.

Then, as he carried her from the Chapel, he saw by her eyes that she was conscious.

At the same time he knew from the stiffness of her body that something had made her immobile and he was also surprised that she had not screamed.

They reached the window through which they had

entered and Pierre said,

"I think that there must be a door to the right of this room that opens into the garden."

"I'll look," Jacques answered.

He left the Banqueting Room and a moment later put his head round the door to say,

"There is, I've opened it,"

Pierre followed him and they were all three in the garden.

They had told the *voiture* they had travelled in from the Left Bank to the *Avenue du Bois* to wait for them a little way down the road and Pierre was thankful to see that his instructions had been obeyed.

He lifted Vada inside and, wrapping the silk vestment even more tightly around her, he held her close in his arms.

"Where do you want to go?" Jacques asked.

"To the studio," Pierre replied.

Jacques closed the door.

"I'm not coming with you," he said through the open window. "I'm going to watch these *sales cochons*. It'll be useful to know who they are for a future occasion."

"Don't fight them," Pierre cautioned. "I don't wish this lady to be involved in any scandal."

"They shall go free because you ask for it," Jacques replied, "but my friends and I will add them to our list of expendable vermin!"

He gave the *cocher* the address of Pierre's studio and raised his arm in salute as the carriage drove away.

Pierre held Vada even closer against him.

"It's all right, my precious darling," he whispered. "You are safe!"

By the light of the street lamps he saw her eyes flicker

and he realised that, while she understood what he was saying, she could not speak.

Her hair had been unfastened and it fell over the outside of the silk vestment and against his shoulders.

He kissed it and then said,

"It's all my fault! I should never have allowed you to dine with Guaita. I did not know then that he had left the Order of the Rosy Cross."

Vada heard what he said, but she found it difficult to think of anything except that she was safe.

Her prayers had been answered.

Pierre had come!

He had saved her!

The terror of the Black Mass being said over her naked body, the horror of the hands turned downwards above her and the evil encroaching like the incense upon her senses had been dissipated.

She was safe!

She was with Pierre and nothing else was of any consequence!

She felt for the moment that she need no longer struggle back to consciousness, no longer notice what was taking place around her!

Afterwards she had very little memory of what happened next until she felt herself being carried up the narrow stairs to Pierre's studio.

The *cocher* went ahead to open the door for them and Pierre carried Vada inside and laid her on the bed.

The room was in darkness save that the window was uncurtained, and through the glass she could see the stars shining in the sky.

Pierre paid the *cocher* and lit the oil lamp.

~163~

Once the studio was illuminated with its golden glow, he came across to the bed to stand for a moment looking down at her.

"Now, my darling." he said gently, "we must make you come alive again. And I cannot bear to see you wearing a garment that has been worn by those appalling blasphemers."

He picked her up in his arms again and Vada wondered what he was going to do with her.

He pulled back the bedclothes and laid her inside the bed, covering her gently with the sheets and blankets.

Then he drew away the silken vestment in such a manner that at no time was her nakedness exposed to him.

He tucked the sheet close up against her chin and said,

"I am going to make you some coffee in my small kitchen. I shall only be a few minutes."

He went away taking the robe with him.

Vada could hear the sound of water being run from a tap and the rattle of cups.

She wondered how long it would be before she regained any feeling in her body.

She tried to move her arms, but it was impossible.

She attempted to speak but no sound would come.

At least, when it seemed to her that Pierre had been gone a long time, he came back to the bedside and set down a cup of black coffee on a small table.

"Now I am going to feed you," he said gently, as if speaking to a child. "I want you to try and swallow the coffee, my precious one, because it will help to destroy the drug they have given you."

As he spoke, he sat down on the bed with his back against the pillows. Very gently he put his left arm round

~164~

Vada's shoulders and pulled her close to him.

Filling a teaspoon with coffee, he held it to her mouth.

For a moment she thought that it would be impossible for the coffee to pass through her lips and yet somehow Pierre managed it.

She could feel the liquid against her tongue and just managed to swallow it, conscious of the heat of it moving down her throat.

Slowly and patiently, Pierre fed her spoonful after spoonful until at last half the cup was empty.

Vada drew in her breath.

"Pier-re!" she managed to murmur.

Her voice sounded very strange and faint and yet it was a tremendous achievement.

Pierre's arm tightened about her.

"You can speak!" he cried excitedly. "That is wonderful, my sweet! Try again! Go on trying!"

An hour later Vada found that feeling was coming back into her body.

First she could turn her head and then she could move her fingers and finally her whole arm.

She had never imagined that any man could be as kind and gentle as Pierre.

He brought her more coffee and finally a small glass of brandy diluted with water.

Because she was so happy to be close to him and to know that he was looking after her, she was no longer frightened by the numbness of her limbs.

Yet there were still fears at the back of her mind as she remembered what had happened.

"What – were they trying to – do to me?" she asked when at last she could make a full sentence.

"I learnt from a man called Léo Taxil, who has for a number of years been exposing Black Magic in France, that Guaita has been attempting to draw the soul or spirit from a body and replace it with that of an elemental."

"Is it possible to – do such a – thing?" Vada whispered.

"Of course not!" Pierre averred positively, "but when Satanists are drugged and have also drunk a great deal of wine, they have hallucinations and they see many of the things they wish to see."

"They were – calling for the – Devil," Vada said with a tremor in her voice.

"You should not have been conscious," Pierre said. "How was that?"

"The wine they – made me – drink tasted so – horrible and I was – afraid of – drinking too much," Vada explained.

She paused and then speaking slowly and with difficulty told him how she had deceived the Marquis and his friends into thinking that she had drunk all the wine by pretending that she had seen a bird on the other side of the room.

"I spilt more of the – wine onto the – floor," she went on, "but there were a few drops left in the – bottom of the – goblet and I drank them because I – felt it seemed so – rude not to do what they – asked of me."

"You were clever, very clever, *ma petite*," Pierre said. "But perhaps it would have been better if you had become completely unconscious. I would still have rescued you."

"I prayed for – God's protection and for – you," Vada replied.

"And your prayers were answered. In fact, my darling,

your Guardian Angel must have been working very hard this evening, for it was just by chance that I went to the *Soleil d'Or* to see Deschamps!"

He drew in his breath.

"I so nearly went home after I had dined at *Chez Louis.*"

"Perhaps – instinctively you – knew that I would – need you," Vada said.

"If my instinct had been working properly. I should not have let you go with Guaita in the first place."

"But – now I am – safe!"

It was a statement rather than a question and Pierre answered,

"You are safe – completely safe. That I promise you."

There was silence and then Vada said in a low voice,

"You don't think that – they could have – done – anything to me? I was – afraid of them."

"There is nothing they can do to you mentally unless you let them," Pierre replied. "I have always been convinced that many people who believe they are possessed by the Devil have only been driven mad by the excesses they have indulged in or perhaps because they have been feeble-minded since birth."

He paused to add,

"A normal intelligent person like you could not be affected by any magic that the Satanists or anyone else for that matter, can conjure up."

"Are – you – sure?" Vada asked.

"Quite sure!"

He held her a little closer before he went on,

"There is one thing that we all know is stronger than evil and against which no Black Magic in the world can prevail."

"What is – that?" Vada asked.

"Love!" Pierre answered. "And because I think you love me a little, *ma belle*, I want you to promise me that you will try to forget what has happened tonight and to remember it will only worry you in the future and will in fact give it an undue importance."

He kissed her forehead before he continued,

"I want you to remember instead that you are here with me. We are close to each other and nothing else matters except our love."

The depth and sincerity in his voice made Vada vibrate to him as she had done before.

She felt as if he was sweeping away the last remnants of the drug that had held her captive and was drawing her into the sunshine.

It was all the more intense because yesterday she had been afraid that she might have lost him.

"I love you – Pierre!" she whispered.

Then very gently, as if he was afraid to hurt her, Pierre bent his head and found her lips.

It was a tender kiss that he might have given to a child.

Vada closed her eyes at the wonder of it and the knowledge that once again he was loving her and had forgotten that they were only to be friends.

Yet, while she wanted Pierre to hold her closer and still closer, he raised his head and said,

"Now we have to plan how I can take you back to the hotel."

For a moment Vada felt wildly disappointed because he would not go on kissing her and then she forced herself to say,

"I don't – think I can – walk."

"I will carry you," Pierre answered. "Equally the night porter at the *Hotel Meurice* might think it strange if I take you back unclothed!"

Vada gave a faint little laugh.

"Not half as – shocked as Charity will be when she – finds that my gown has – disappeared!"

"That's a problem for tomorrow morning," Pierre said. "We must deal first with tonight's."

He moved his arm from behind Vada's back and she wanted to cry out because she wished above all else to stay close to him.

"You must forgive me if I leave you for a few moments," Pierre said. "I have a friend in the building, who I know will lend you one of her dresses."

He stood up and smiled down at Vada.

"Don't fly away before I come back. You do such unpredictable things, I am afraid to let you out of my sight!"

"I will – wait for you, Pierre," Vada promised.

She watched him cross the room and thought that her words could be prophetic.

How wonderful it would be if she could stay here in the studio with Pierre and know that when he came home she would be waiting for him.

She looked up at the high ceiling, the window overlooking the roofs of Paris and the walls decorated with pictures and told herself that it was the loveliest room she had ever been in.

How could damask, velvet, chandeliers and expensive furnishings be of any significance when a room did not contain love?

It was, Vada thought, her love for Pierre and his for her that made this studio a Palace and made her think that to live here with him would be to find a Paradise all of their own.

'I love him!' Vada told herself, and knew that all she wanted was to be close to him and know that he loved her.

He was gone for some time and she began to be afraid that his lady friend, whoever she might be, had been so charming and so attractive that he was in no hurry to return to her.

'He must know the woman very well!' Vada thought.

She was sure that by now it must be long after midnight and only someone who was a very close friend would not mind being awoken at such an hour with a demand for the loan of a gown.

Perhaps Pierre had loved her once, she tortured herself, and wondered what she was like.

If she was French, she would probably be dark.

Did he perhaps admire dark women more than fair?

She had always believed that Frenchmen preferred blondes in contrast to the women of their own nationality, who were predominantly brunette.

But that was undoubtedly one of the myths that American women blinded themselves with.

Vada was too intelligent not to realise that women pretended a lot of things merely to boost their own ego and persuade themselves that they were more attractive than they really were.

'How can Pierre really love me?' she asked herself in a sudden panic.

Their lives had been so different and he was right in being afraid because they knew so little about each other.

Yet how could she tell him the truth?

She could hear all too clearly the scathing manner in which he had spoken of '*Miss Moneybags*' and '*title-seeking rich American women*'.

His contempt for the very rich and for those who enjoyed nothing but the Social world was very obvious.

Once, when he was talking about the reign of Louis XVI, he said,

"Power, rank and money spoilt the aristocrats, as they still spoil people today."

"Why does it do that?" Vada asked.

"Because it isolates them from reality, from physical suffering and the need to struggle."

"And those things are important?"

"I think so," Pierre replied. "Man must strive, not only for material necessities but to prove himself."

"And the – rich do not – have to do – that?"

"No, they sweep past in their luxurious carriages unaware of those they splatter with mud. They see life from behind a protective glass window and most of them are made of cardboard."

There was a contempt in Pierre's voice that Vada could not ignore.

Once again it seemed to her that she was imprisoned by the gold chains that had kept her captive all her life.

Then she knew that Pierre loved her for herself, the unimportant, poor companion, the girl who was of so little consequence that she was not even chaperoned in Paris.

'He must never know the truth,' she told herself frantically. 'If I lose his love, then I lose everything that matters to me.'

Even as she thought of him, he came back into the

room carrying a gown over his arm.

Of a black and white material, its tight bodice contrasted with the frilled skirt. There were tiny touches of red at the neck and sleeves, which gave it that indefinable *chic* that was the birthright of all Frenchwomen, poor or rich.

"You have been – a long time." Vada said almost accusingly before she could stop herself.

"Were you worried about yourself or about me?" Pierre asked in an amused voice.

Vada hoped that she was still too numb to blush, but she had the idea that Pierre was aware of her jealousy.

"My friend," he said in explanation, "was entertaining someone and I could not interrupt until they had said goodnight."

"I thought you said that it was – wrong to ask a gentleman up to your room at – night," Vada pointed out.

Pierre's eyes were twinkling and, putting the gown on the bed, he sat down facing Vada.

"Are you curious or jealous, my darling?" he asked.

For a moment Vada wanted to lie to him and then she told the truth.

"Both!" she whispered and her eyes fell before his.

He laughed softly and bent forward to kiss her very gently, his lips just brushing hers.

"There is no need for jealousy," he said, "and I will assuage your curiosity. My friend is an actress and lives in a world in which you, if I can prevent it, will never become involved."

He smiled and added,

"At the same time she is a generous kind person who is always ready to help those in need. So she has lent me one of her prettiest dresses."

He stood up as he spoke and, taking the gown, opened it.

"Sit up!" he ordered.

Vada did as she was told, holding the sheet close against her breasts.

Pierre put the dress over her head and she slipped her arms into it.

"I will do it up for you," he offered.

She bent forward and he buttoned the gown across her back.

When he had finished, the full skirt was spread out in front of Vada over the sheet.

"Now I am going to help you to edge yourself to the side of the bed," Pierre said. "If you sit there, I will put on your feet a pair of slippers I have brought that I think will fit you."

Vada did as he suggested and, although it was still very difficult for her to move her legs, she finally managed to put first one small foot and then the other onto the rug at the side of the bed.

Pierre knelt down at her feet and put the black slippers he had brought on the rug beside her.

"My feet still feel as though they don't belong to me," Vada murmured.

Pierre took her right foot in his hand and looked down at the small pink-tipped toes and the high instep.

It was an exquisitely shaped little foot and he held it in both his hands before he said in a low voice,

"Perhaps then I should make it mine!"

He bent forward and kissed it.

His action was unexpected. Vada could feel the

pressure of his lips on her skin and felt herself thrill.

"I would rather you – kissed my – mouth," she whispered shyly.

"I want to kiss all of you," he answered, "I want to be sure that every precious part of you, my dearest love, belongs to me."

He looked up as he spoke. In the lamplight Vada saw the fire in his eyes that had been there the first night he brought her to the studio.

Yet now it seemed to her that it was different.

The fire was there, but she was no longer afraid.

Instead she felt as if it was a part of herself, part of the flame that he had awoken in her and which she knew was the flame of love.

With an effort Pierre took his eyes from hers and slipped on one of the slippers he had brought for her.

It was just a little too large.

He kissed her left foot before fitting the other.

Then he rose to his feet and smiled at her.

"Now," he said, "we have to do something about your hair."

Vada put up her hands a little uncertainly.

She had forgotten that her hair was loose.

Fair, like sunshine in the light from the lamps, it fell over her shoulders nearly to her waist.

"I suppose my hairpins – are all left – behind with my clothes," she said.

"That is something I did not think of," Pierre said, "and I don't like to disturb my friend again."

"No – please – don't," Vada begged him.

He walked across the room to the chest of drawers.

"If I tie it back with ribbon," he said, "you will look

~174~

quite respectable."

He opened a drawer and after a moment he said,

"In case you are still being suspicious about me, I don't possess a woman's ribbon, but I think one of my ties will pass muster."

He came back with a black silk tie in his hand.

Sweeping Vada's hair away from her shoulders, he gathered it at the nape of her neck and tied it in a bow.

"Now you look very young and very lovely," he said. "I would like to paint you like that."

"Will you?" Vada asked.

"One day I will paint you a hundred times," he replied. "And I do prefer that glorious hair of yours hanging over your shoulders as it was just now."

There was something in the depth of his voice that made Vada blush a little.

Then once again in that abrupt manner he used when he appeared to call himself to attention, Pierre said,

"I am going out to the street to find a *voiture*. I will not be long. There are usually plenty about at this time of the night."

He did not look at her again, but went from the studio and Vada listened to his steps going down the uncarpeted stairs.

She wanted desperately not to go away, but to stay where she was.

Why must she leave Pierre and go back to the hotel?

Why should she not stay here in his arms and listen to his words of love?

She thought of how he had kissed her feet and felt herself quiver inside.

What other man could be so passionate and at the

same time so tender? So gentle and yet so masterful?

'Even if I knew a thousand men,' Vada thought, 'there would never be anyone like Pierre.'

He was the man she loved, the man she wanted, the man who in her dreams she had been seeking ever since she had been old enough to think about love.

The love that her mother had told her would never be hers, the love she thought that she must be denied because of her wealth.

"I love him!" she whispered.

Even as she said the words she knew that she would fight to keep him. She would do anything to avoid losing either him or the love he had for her.

She was not certain how it could be done, but the only thing that mattered in her life now or in the future was to keep Pierre.

'He must never find out about me,' she told herself.

She heard him coming back up the stairs and waited with a light in her eyes until the moment that he actually stepped into the studio.

Then, because she could not help it, she held out her arms.

He crossed the room to her to look down at her upturned face and at the invitation in her eyes.

Then he went down on one knee beside her and took her in his arms.

He kissed her passionately as if he could not help himself.

Later, while she was still clinging to him, her arms around his neck with her lips soft beneath his, he raised his head to say a little unsteadily,

"If anyone uses magic, it is you!"

~176~

"Good – magic?"

"Wonderful magic! And your spell, my little White Witch, is almost inescapable!"

"Al-most?" Vada questioned against his mouth.

He kissed her again and then he said,

"Come along, the carriage is waiting and we are not millionaires. The *cocher* charges an inordinate amount of *sous* all the time he and his horse are standing there doing nothing."

Vada wanted to cry out that she could buy a thousand *voitures* and not notice the cost!

But because she was afraid of losing Pierre, who had obviously forgotten all his ideas of taking things slowly and with caution, she said quickly,

"We must not be – extravagant."

"Except with kisses." Pierre answered. "I like you to be a spendthrift with them as long as they are given to me!"

He kissed her again and then lifted her up in his arms.

When he reached the door, Vada said,

"You have forgotten to turn out the lamp."

"I do not intend to be away long," he answered, a touch of severity in his voice.

She gave a faint little laugh and said,

"Tonight – you will have to – come up the stairs with me."

"I suppose you think you have won a moral victory?" he said.

"No," she answered, "I am only delighted because I shall be able to keep you with me – a little longer."

His arms tightened instinctively about her and she hoped that he was going to kiss her.

Instead he proceeded carefully down the stairs and,

when they reached the road, he lifted her gently into the *voiture*.

He gave the address to the *cocher* and climbed in beside her.

She turned towards him and he took her once again into his arms.

"When you arrive home," he said, "you must promise me to try to sleep and not to think about anything except that we have been happy together this last hour or so."

"Very – very happy," Vada said. "It was worth everything to find out that after all – you are a Symbolist!"

Pierre laughed and then he said,

"Tomorrow you are to stay in bed. If you feel at all ill, you must send for a doctor."

Vada was surprised, but he went on,

"There is no need for you to tell him too much. Just say you drank some wine which you think must have been bad and which made you lose your balance."

"I shall be all right," Vada said firmly. "I have no wish to see a doctor."

"Then at least try to sleep late," Pierre insisted. "You could leave a note for Charity not to awaken you."

"Yes, I will do that," Vada agreed. "But how am I going to explain to her that I have come back in a strange dress?"

Pierre thought for a moment, and then he said,

"There could have been an accident with a pot of coffee. It is something I saw happen not so very long ago and it soaked through everything the woman was wearing at the time."

"Yes, that's a good idea," Vada said, "and that is why I had to borrow a dress from a friend."

"I will collect the gown and shoes when I come to see you tomorrow," Pierre said. "Then we can make our plans."

"What plans?" Vada asked.

They were moving down the *Quai de Louvre* and she thought unhappily that in a few moments they would reach the hotel.

"I don't wish to trouble you with that tonight," Pierre answered.

But Vada was curious.

She raised her head from his shoulder to look up at him. In the light from the street-lamps she thought how handsome he looked and how different from any other man she had ever seen.

"Tell me!" she pleaded.

"Plans about ourselves," he said evasively.

"Tell me or I shall lie awake all night wondering what they are," Vada insisted.

"That is an unfair argument and you well know it!" he replied. "You have a crafty way of getting what you want, little Vada!"

"Perhaps it is just – that I am feminine!" she answered.

He laughed softly and kissed her cheek.

"As you are so persistent – we have to talk about getting married!"

Vada was still.

"You don't think that I can allow you to get into any more trouble?" he asked. "I want to look after you and much the easiest and best way is for you to be my wife."

For a moment Vada felt as if she could not think, could not find words to answer him and then she said in a very small voice,

"But I thought that you had no – wish to be married, that you wanted – to be free."

"That is what I told myself," Pierre answered. "I had chosen my way of life and I enjoyed it. I was extremely happy in it."

He paused for a moment before he went on,

"I am not pretending, Vada, that there have not been other women in my life, but never, and this is the truth, never have I wanted to marry anyone until I met you."

"Are you – are you – sure?" Vada stammered.

"More sure about this than I have ever been about anything else," Pierre answered. "That is why I wanted us to get to know each other a little better and to have time to think. But that time has passed."

His arms tightened as he went on,

"I never knew I could suffer such agonies as I suffered this evening when I realised what was happening to you and it seemed to take several centuries of time to travel from the *Soleil d'Or* to the *Avenue du Bois.*"

His voice deepened as he continued,

"I knew then that you were everything that mattered to me in life. You belong to me. I intend to look after you, protect you and love you!"

He felt Vada quiver and he added,

"I did not mean to tell you this tonight, my precious. We will work out all the details tomorrow. Go to bed now and remember only that you are mine and I adore you."

He put his hand under her chin as he spoke and his lips were on hers.

His kiss was possessive and demanding, but there was also, Vada felt, a dedication in it as if he offered her not only his heart but his soul.

He felt her lips respond to his and she knew that there was a thankfulness rising within her because he loved her and she loved him.

This was the love that drew two people together and made them one.

This was the love that transcended the confines of the body and became part of the mystic spiritual wonder of music, poetry and of all beauty.

"I love you!" Pierre said in his deep voice, "and, when you are my wife, you will realise how much!"

It was a physical agony to realise that the carriage had come to a standstill and they had now reached the *Hotel Meurice*.

The porter came hurrying down to open the door of the carriage.

"I am afraid Miss Sparling has wrenched her ankle," Pierre explained in his ordinary voice. "I must carry her into the hotel and up the stairs."

"I'll work the lift for you, *monsieur*," the porter suggested.

"That would be very helpful," Pierre replied.

The porter collected the key from the desk and took them up in the lift.

Vada laid her head against Pierre's shoulder,

'It cannot be true!' she thought.

She must have imagined the things he had said to her in the carriage and yet she knew that they were engraved upon her heart.

The lift stopped at the third floor.

Pierre waited while the porter opened the outside door of the suite and switched on the lights.

He carried Vada into her bedroom and set her down

against the soft pillows under the draped satin canopy.

It was all very rich and luxurious in contrast with the austerity of the studio, yet it was with difficulty that Vada prevented herself from holding onto Pierre and begging him to take her back.

"Do you think you can manage?" he asked as the porter withdrew.

"Yes, of course," she answered.

He picked up her nightgown, which was lying on a chair, and put it beside her on the bed.

"Shall I undo your dress?" he asked.

"Perhaps the top buttons," she answered, "they are always the most difficult – "

She sat up and bent forward and he undid the small black buttons as far as her waist.

'We might already be husband and wife,' she thought.

They were so close, already a part of each other, that the Marriage Ceremony would only bring the Blessing of God to what was already a perfect union.

"Thank – you," Vada smiled as Pierre finished and she raised her face to his.

"Goodnight, my darling," he said in his deep voice. "I will come and see you at about noon tomorrow and, if you are well enough, I will take you out to luncheon."

"I shall be counting the minutes until I see you again."

His lips held hers for what seemed to her an all too brief moment. Then with a smile he left her, closing the door gently behind him.

Vada lay back among the pillows.

He loved her! He wanted to marry her!

She was to be his wife!

It seemed so overwhelming, so tremendous that she

~182~

could hardly credit the truth of what he had said in the carriage.

Then she realised with a sudden sinking of her heart that she could not many Pierre while she was still committed to the Duke.

First she must be free or she could not go to her Wedding with a clear conscience.

She tried to fight against the inner knowledge that this must be the right thing to do and yet insistently her conscience would not be assuaged.

She might deceive Pierre about her identity, although she had the uncomfortable feeling that she would have to be married in her rightful name or it would not be legal! But before they could plan their Wedding day, she must disencumber herself from her past.

She must be free from the ties of another marriage that had been planned for her because of her wealth and which now she knew would have been a travesty of all that was holy and all that was sacred.

Vada closed her eyes.

It was going to be hard, but somehow she must find the strength to do what she knew to be right.

Chapter Eight

Vada rang for Charity at six o'clock in the morning.

When the old maid came hurrying into her bedroom to see if anything was wrong, she told her,

"Will you start packing at once, Charity? We are leaving for England."

Charity appeared to be about to argue, but then she said,

"And a very good thing too if you ask me, Miss Vada! The sooner we get to England, the sooner we can go back to America and that's where I want to be."

Vada had anticipated that Charity might make a fuss about having so little time in which to pack.

But with the assistance of two chambermaids, they were able to drive off to the Station to catch a train for Calais that left at nine o'clock.

What was far more difficult was that Vada had to write a letter to Pierre, which would be given to him when he called at noon.

She did not feel ill, although she had a headache and her legs were a trifle unsteady, but it was extremely difficult to find the right words with which to express herself.

She did not wish to upset Pierre or make him anxious about her.

At the same time she knew that she could not tell him to his face that she was going away.

Somehow it would be impossible, if he questioned her closely, for her to lie or to prevent him from learning the truth.

Having dressed herself in her travelling gown, Vada

sat down at the desk in the sitting room, hearing the murmur of Charity's voice as she ordered around the two chambermaids.

There was also the rustle of tissue paper as they packed her elegant Worth gowns in trunks that she had brought from America half-empty.

She thought of telling Charity not to pack everything, as they would be returning to Paris, but she thought that would evoke too many questions.

It would certainly sweep away the satisfaction Charity felt in believing that she would soon be returning to America.

'She will go, but I will stay behind,' Vada said to herself.

Then almost for the first time she thought of her mother and felt afraid.

She had been swept along on the tide of her love for Pierre without really considering that it must end in marriage.

It had really been quite a shock to her last night when he had said,

"I want to look after you and much the easiest and best way is for you to be my wife."

It had been inevitable, she thought now, from the first.

Yet strangely enough she had been content just to be with him, to know that he loved her and most of all to feel his lips on hers.

She had never imagined, even to herself, that they would be married and perhaps live in his studio so that she could look after him as he intended to look after her.

Now it seemed to her that nothing in life could be more wonderful, yet she was not so foolish as not to realise there were many difficulties ahead.

Her mother would be furious! Vada could not pretend to herself about that!

She had set her heart on seeing her daughter a Duchess.

It was not only that she was a snob, like all her generation, in believing that a title was all-important.

It was also, Vada knew, because her mother sincerely believed that it was the only way her daughter would find happiness.

Vada remembered the conversation she had with her mother when she had said that no one would love her for herself alone and there was no man in America who was her equal.

'Pierre loves me for myself!' Vada cried out in her heart.

She felt a little quiver run through her because it was so miraculous to know that he wished to marry her knowing nothing about her, loving her because he could not help himself.

Then, almost as menacingly as the black bat that had hovered over her like an evil omen last night, there was the question of what Pierre would think about it when he knew how rich she was?

'He must not know. I cannot tell him until it is too late for him to do anything about it,' Vada thought frantically.

She picked up the pen and in her well-shaped elegant hand she wrote,

"Pierre.
I have to go to England and it is something I
cannot refuse to do. I will, however, return in three days'

*time and then I shall be free to be with you, which is
what I want more than anything else in the whole world.
Vada."*

There were so much else that she wanted to say, so
many ways in which she longed to express her love.

Almost like a poem, words came into her mind and
then she recognised that it would be better to write as little
as possible.

Pierre inevitably would be curious, to say the least of
it!

He would demand answers to his questions and it
would be soon enough to face that difficulty when she
could return to him free of her obligation to the Duke.

Unable to sleep during the night she had played with
the idea of writing to the Duke, telling him that she had
fallen in love and that there was no point in even meeting
him.

Then she was aware that this was the cowardly way
out.

Besides there was always the chance that the Duke
might try, as her mother most certainly would, to prevent
her from marrying Pierre.

It would be safer if she told him the truth, threw
herself on his mercy and begged him, if he would not help
her, at least not to obstruct her from marrying the man she
loved.

As she wrote Pierre's name on it, she had the impulse
to kiss the letter because he would open it. Then she told
herself that this was a moment when she must be practical
and not sentimental.

With her own hands she packed the gown that Pierre

had borrowed for her last night and the black slippers.

She put them into one of the Worth boxes, which had been emptied of an expensive gown that she had ordered and wrote his name on the box.

In order to prevent Charity from seeing it, she rang for a pageboy and had both the box and the letter taken downstairs to the reception desk to await Pierre's arrival.

She was half-afraid that, because he might be impatient to see her despite the fact that he had told her to sleep late, he would arrive before they left.

She gave a little sigh of relief when at last the carriage, piled high with their trunks, carried Charity and herself into the *Place Vendôme* and up the *Rue de la Paix* on the way to the *Gare du Nord*.

As they passed Worth's shop, Vada could not help thinking with a little smile that never again would she buy the expensive gowns that her mother had thought so important to her trousseau.

Even if Pierre should let her spend her money on such frivolities, which she doubted, they would certainly not be suitable for the wife of a poor writer living on the Left Bank.

She thought of the black and white cotton gown that she had just packed up for Pierre's friend.

It could not have been expensive and yet it had been smart and elegant. Vada knew that she must learn to buy economically and still look attractive because she wanted Pierre to admire her.

Everything in the future seemed golden because she would be with him.

Everything seemed touched with an enchantment that made it difficult to think of anything but his eyes gazing into hers and his lips touching her mouth.

'I love him more every moment!' Vada murmured to herself and started when Charity asked,

"Did you speak, Miss Vada?"

"Only to myself," Vada answered.

"You're looking better this morning," Charity said, "despite the fact that you were out again last night."

Vada did not answer and she went on,

"I was worried about you yesterday morning, I was really! I've never known you to be so listless and depressed. I couldn't think what'd come over you."

"I am all right now," Vada assured her.

It was true, she thought!

Despite what she had been through with the Satanists, despite the effects of the drugged wine, she felt well.

It was, of course, because she was happy and because Pierre had brought her back to life in more ways than one.

All the long hours that they journeyed to Calais, Vada could only think of Pierre.

It was with a little tremor of fear that she hoped he would not be too angry when he received her letter.

Then she told herself that he would suppose that Miss Holtz had sent for her and she had to obey the summons.

She could have given him that explanation, but she could not lie.

Instead, she only hoped that he would be deceived into believing that she had gone at Miss Holtz's command to tell her that her position as her companion was at an end.

'That is what he will think,' Vada told herself, 'and that is what he must believe until the very last moment.'

She could not help feeling frightened of what would

happen when eventually she confessed to Pierre who she really was.

Then she tried to convince herself that it was completely unimportant beside the magnitude of their love.

Love was not something that you could turn off like a light because of being upset or annoyed.

As Verlaine had said, *"Love always rises like a flame"*.

Then it became a fire?

That is what had happened to her and she had seen the fire in Pierre's eyes.

A fire that excited her and she was no longer afraid of it!

*

They reached Calais at two o'clock in the afternoon and the ferry to Dover was waiting.

The crossing took only three hours. Vada had sent a telegram, as Nancy Sparling had told her to do, to the Dowager Duchess, so that there was a Courier waiting for them at Dover.

"I've engaged a carriage for you, Miss Holtz, in the train that will be leaving almost immediately," he said. "If you'll wait there with your maid, I'll see to your luggage."

Every comfort was provided in the carriage.

There was a huge hamper filled with delicacies of every sort, besides a half bottle of champagne and a half bottle of hock.

There was a hay-basket containing a pot of hot tea, which delighted Charity.

There were rugs for their knees and at least a dozen

magazines and all the day's newspapers.

Finally the Courier returned just before the train started to say that their luggage was in the van and they would be stopping at the Duke's private Station halfway to London, where a carriage would be waiting for them.

"How far is The Castle from the Station?" Vada asked.

"Under an hour's drive," the Courier replied. "His Grace's carriage has been specially built for travelling at speed and I am certain that you will find it very comfortable."

"I am sure I shall," Vada answered with a little smile.

The Courier bowed and left them to find his own carriage.

Vada was not hungry, but she ate a little of the food that was provided in the hamper, whilst Charity drank the tea with relish.

"You're very silent, Miss Vada," she commented after a little while.

"I was thinking," Vada replied.

"Now don't go upsetting yourself!" Charity admonished. "Your mother knows what's best for you and in making her arrangements has thought only of your happiness."

"Yes, I know."

It was worrying to think how angry and disappointed her mother would be, but much worse to plan what she would say to the Duke.

She must try to make him understand, but how?

'If only Pierre could do it for me,' she mused.

But this was one challenge that she must face herself and after all, had she not always believed that Americans were brave and self-reliant?

Had not Nancy Sparling told her that she must learn to stand on her own two feet?

Vada gave a deep sigh.

When this was over, Pierre would look after her and protect her, and she need have no more worries or fears for the future.

He could be kind and gentle and she knew also that he was very masterful.

There was something authoritative about him, something she knew would make her always obey him, not only because she would wish to do so, but also because he was the sort of man who commanded obedience.

'Everything about him is right,' she thought. 'He is so masculine, so much a man and yet no one could be more tender.'

She remembered how he had fed her last night, how he had tied her hair back, buttoned up her dress and she closed her eyes because even to think of it made her thrill.

Because she was thinking of Pierre, the time in the train passed quickly and then there was the drive of an hour across country to the Duke's Castle.

The Courier had not exaggerated when he had said that the carriage was very comfortable.

It was specially sprung so that even the roughest of roads seemed smooth and the team of four magnificent chestnuts went at what seemed to Vada an almost incredible speed.

They finally turned in through two huge wrought iron gates with great stone heraldic lions on either side of them.

Vada saw a long drive and, at the end of it in the dusk, The Castle.

Built and re-built over the centuries, it had an

unexpected Fairy-like quality.

Now grey against the evening sky, its beauty seemed to blend with the trees, the landscape and the lake.

The mullioned windows caught the last rays of the setting sun and shimmered iridescently as the carriage drew nearer.

As they drew up in front of a flight of steps, the doors were opened and a warm golden light streamed out as if in welcome.

A little dazed from the speed they had travelled at, Vada stepped out to be greeted by a butler with all the courtesy of a polished Diplomat.

"May I welcome you, miss, to Grantham Castle," he intoned. "Her Grace is expecting you."

He led Vada across an enormous marble hall hung with ancient flags and decorated with suits of armour.

He opened the door of a large drawing room and for a moment Vada could see only glittering chandeliers, the reflection of mirror in mirror, pictures and a profusion of hothouse plants.

Then, at the far end of the room seated in front of a magnificent marble mantelshelf, she saw the Dowager Duchess.

The Duchess rose. She was slim and graceful despite her years and she moved towards Vada with both hands outstretched.

"My dear child," she said, "I am so delighted to see you!"

She must have been a beautiful woman in her youth for there were still remnants in the straight aristocratic nose and deep-set eyes.

She wore black and there were six strings of superb

pearls round her neck, while diamonds and pearls glittered in her ears.

"You have had a good journey and they looked after you when you arrived at Dover?" she asked.

"Everything was perfect, thank you," Vada replied shyly.

"You must be tired," the Duchess said, "and I am sure too that you are hungry. I have ordered dinner much later than usual, so that you will have time for a bath and to change without hurrying."

The Duchess gave a little laugh.

"Nothing is more infuriating than to have to hurry as soon as one has arrived at one's destination."

She smiled again at Vada and added,

"I hope you managed to find the most delectable gowns in Paris. Your mother told me that you were to buy most of your trousseau from the redoubtable Mr. Worth. He is indeed a genius."

Vada felt uncomfortable at the mention of the word 'trousseau', but she had decided that she would say nothing to the Duchess about her decision not to marry her son.

It was her mother and the Duchess who had arranged it between them.

She had the idea that, if the Duchess thought that she was going to upset their plans, she would make trouble.

Almost as if the elder woman sensed that Vada was thinking about her son, she said,

"I am afraid that you will not see the Duke this evening. He had to go to London unexpectedly yesterday, but he is arriving back first thing tomorrow. Then you will meet each other."

At first Vada felt a momentary sense of relief.

Then she thought that this would mean she might have to stay longer than she had intended.

She had told herself during the journey that if she was clever she might be able to tell the Duke tonight that she could not marry him and then she would be able to return to Paris tomorrow.

This was now impossible and her sense of relief was quickly replaced by one of anxiety.

She wondered whether, if she had to stay until the day after tomorrow, it would be possible to send Pierre a telegram.

Perhaps the Duke would allow her to do that.

While she was thinking, the Duchess was drawing her down the room towards the hall.

"There is so much for you to learn about the house and its history," she was saying as they walked towards the great carved staircase. "The Castle is very large. I remember when I came here as a bride that I felt almost overpowered by it, but it has a friendly atmosphere, which I know you will find as I did."

"'It's very beautiful," Vada managed to say.

"That is what I hoped you would think," the Dowager approved. "It is a heritage that passes through the family from generation to generation and to which everyone in turn contributes something."

She paused half-way up the staircase to point at the opposite wall.

"The flag hanging there," she said, "is the one my son's ancestor brought back from Waterloo and the one on the right of it was captured by another of the family who served with the Duke of Marlborough."

'I should be so thrilled by it all,' Vada thought to

herself, 'if it was going to mean something to me.'

She loved history and one reason why she had always wanted to visit England was because it was so full of all the things she had learnt about in her history books.

But now she would be living in France and English history would not concern her.

"I think you will like your bedroom," the Duchess was saying in her quiet musical voice. "It is known as the 'Queen's room' and every bride who comes to this Castle sleeps there."

Vada wondered what the Duchess would think if she knew that she was in effect an impostor.

She had no right to the 'Queen's room', but this was not the moment to say so.

Charity was there already, supervising two housemaids in starched caps and flowing white aprons who were unpacking.

They rose as the Duchess entered and dropped a curtsey and Charity, for the moment forgetting her American independence, did likewise.

"I have told Miss Holtz," the Duchess said to Charity, "that she has plenty of time to change. Dinner has been put back to nine o'clock."

"It's very kind of you," Vada said.

"All we want to do, my dear," the Duchess replied, "is to make you feel happy and *at home*."

She seemed to accentuate the last words and then she went from the bedroom leaving Vada with the maids.

Vada anticipated while she was bathing and changing for dinner that she would be alone at dinner with the Duchess and felt that it might be uncomfortable if they were to talk about her engagement, her trousseau and the

Wedding.

She need not have worried.

When she came downstairs a few minutes before nine o'clock, it was to find a number of people assembled in the drawing room.

There was the Duke's private Chaplain, the Duchess's companion, a charming woman of over fifty, and a married couple who were the Duke's cousins and were staying in The Castle.

It seemed to Vada that they could not repress the curiosity in their eyes when they looked at her.

At the same time they treated her with a well-bred courtesy and nothing they said could possibly be construed as embarrassing.

Because the Duchess felt Vada must be tired, they all retired to bed soon after dinner.

Only when she was alone in the four-poster bed in the 'Queen's room' did Vada feel once again that she was an impostor.

'When I see the Duke, I will explain everything to him,' she told herself, 'and then I can go back to Paris.'

There were pictures of the Duke all over the house.

That he was fair-haired and blue-eyed and very obviously an English aristocrat could be seen in every portrait.

The Duchess had proudly shown her one of him wearing Peer's robes, which Vada thought made him look older and rather awe-inspiring as she knew that a portrait that portrays a person's best features seldom shows their character or personality.

Certainly the Duke's pictures gave her no hint as to what kind of man he was and whether he would understand that she could not marry him.

She wondered if he would be very incensed at the thought of losing all her money. If so, would it not be possible for her to give him what he obviously craved?

It might be a solution of what to do with her millions.

The mere thought of all her wealth made Vada feel so afraid that she trembled.

It seemed an absurd paradox that she had to explain to the Duke that he could not have her money, which would upset him, and to Pierre that she had so much money, which he despised.

'It will be all right. I am sure it will be all right,' she tried to console herself.

But only because she was so tired after all she had been through the night before and because of the long journey, did she finally stop worrying by falling asleep.

*

She awoke in the morning with a new buoyancy.

The effects of the drug given her by the Marquis had at last worn off and she could not help being intrigued by The Castle and the treasures in it.

'I shall never see them again, so I might as well enjoy them while I am here,' she told herself.

She remembered that it was more or less the same thing she had said to herself in Paris when she had wanted to go first to the *Soleil d'Or* and then to the *Moulin Rouge*.

The last visit had been disastrous, not only because she had been shocked but because of the effect her innocence and lack of sophistication had on the Marquis.

But she was determined to obey Pierre not to think

about the Marquis or the Black Mass.

The Castle was a page out of history, not one page, but a whole book of them.

The Duchess instructed the Chaplain to show Vada around and she discovered that he was also the Curator and had a love and a deep knowledge of everything that The Castle contained.

He told her stories of the battles the family had fought in since the time of William the Conqueror.

The Grants, for that was the family name, had been Statesmen, politicians, soldiers and explorers and there was even one who had been a pirate at the time of Queen Elizabeth.

"Then they were wealthy with the spoils from the Spanish ships they captured," the Chaplain said with a sigh, "but the money gradually disappeared down the centuries. And now there are so many things that want doing and we just cannot afford to do them."

He spoke as if The Castle and the Grantham estates were part of himself and Vada learnt that this attitude was assumed by everyone connected with the family.

A housemaid said to her,

"We find this room's rather cold, miss, when there's an East wind blowin'."

And the Head Gardener said,

"We'll have the finest crop of peaches this year we've ever had."

There was something rather delightful at the idea that these people all belonged, Vada thought.

She could understand why the Duke wanted to keep up The Castle in the way that his ancestors had been able to do.

'He will find another heiress,' she reassuringly told herself.

She wanted the Duke to be happy, just as she and Pierre would be happy.

She wanted to spread her love and share it with everyone she met. She wanted every story to have a happy ending and everyone to know some of the rapture and wonder that was in her own heart.

The day slipped by quickly and the Duchess and Vada were having tea alone in the drawing room when the Duke walked in.

"You are back, David!" the Duchess exclaimed, rising to her feet. "I hoped that you would catch the early train."

He advanced down the room.

Vada thought that he was in fact very like his portraits, except that he was much thinner and looked considerably older than he had in most of them.

He was very elegant in a grey frock coat that he had worn for his visit to London and, after he had bent to kiss his mother on the cheek, he turned to Vada and held out his hand.

"I must apologise that I was not here to welcome you, Miss Holtz," he said.

There was something kind and friendly in his voice and, as Vada touched his hand, she knew that she was no longer afraid of him.

She had the feeling that he would understand what she had to say.

When he sat down on a chair and started telling his mother something amusing that had happened to him on the journey, she knew that she liked him.

'Perhaps,' she thought to herself, 'if I had not known

Pierre, I would at this moment have been thinking quite seriously that I must do as Mama wished and marry the Duke.'

But having once known love, she knew now that marriage with anyone else but Pierre was impossible for her, however much they might try to persuade her into it.

The Duke drank a cup of tea and the Duchess rose to her feet.

"We have a dinner party tonight," she said. "You must forgive me if I go and lie down. I find parties very tiring unless I rest beforehand."

"I will look after Miss Holtz, Mama," the Duke suggested.

He crossed the room to open the door for his mother.

As he came back, Vada said to him in a breathless voice,

"Could I – talk to – Your Grace?"

"But, of course," he answered. "Shall we go into the library where I usually sit? It's much more comfortable and we shall not be disturbed by the servants coming to clear the tea things away."

"That would be – very nice," Vada said in a small voice.

She followed him through the hall and he took her into the charming and colourful library with books stretching from floor to ceiling and a bow window looking out over the lake.

The room was furnished with a sofa and deep armchairs of red leather.

"Have you been shown around the house?" the Duke asked.

"Your Chaplain took me round," Vada replied. "It's

magnificent."

"I had hoped to do that myself," the Duke said, "but my visit to London was unavoidable and we were not expecting you so soon."

"No," Vada answered, "and that is something – I want to tell Your Grace."

He looked at her searchingly, as if he sensed her nervousness, and then he said,

"Shall we sit down?"

Obediently Vada seated herself on the sofa and the Duke pulled a leather armchair a little nearer so that he was close beside her.

"What is worrying you?" he asked in a kind voice.

"I-I cannot – marry you," Vada blurted out.

The Duke said nothing, but his eyes were on her face as she went on,

"I know that – your mother and – mine arranged it and I – agreed because at the – time there was – nothing else I could do. But now everything has – changed."

"May I ask in what way?" the Duke enquired.

Vada took a deep breath.

"I have – fallen in – love."

The Duke raised his eyebrows.

"You may think it very strange and even I find it difficult to believe – it has happened," she said, "but I met someone in Paris – "

"If I am correct," the Duke interposed, "you have only been in Paris for a few days."

"Yes, I know," Vada answered. "We met each other by chance and, although neither of us meant it to happen, we fell in love."

Her voice trembled for a moment and then her face

suddenly lit up as she said,

"I love him! I love him so much – that I could not contemplate – I could not think of marrying anyone else. Please understand!"

The Duke smiled.

"I do understand," he said. "But does your mother know of this?"

"Mama has no idea," Vada replied. "Even if I had written to her – about it, she would not yet have received the letter. But nothing – she can say or do will stop me!"

"Are you not being a little hasty?" the Duke asked tentatively.

Vada smiled at him.

"I know all the arguments you are going to make," she said, "I have heard them already from the man I love – but they are none of them important."

She paused and went on,

"You may think perhaps that I am too young to know my own mind – but I do know it! I know too that a love like mine for him and his for me is – something that happens once in a lifetime. I cannot risk losing it!"

"What are you going to do?" the Duke asked.

"If you will help me," she said, "I want to go back to Paris at once – tomorrow."

"Alone?" the Duke asked.

"I shall not be alone when I get there," Vada answered. "I am going to get married at once – before anyone can stop me! Before my mother can travel from America to prevent me, as she is certain to try to do, when the Duchess tells her what has happened."

The Duke was silent and then he said,

"You have certainly set me a problem. I don't know

~203~

what I should do in the circumstances."

"Just help me," Vada said, "and – don't try to stop me."

The Duke rose to his feet to walk to the window and gaze into the sunlit garden.

"You are very young," he said in a worried voice.

"But not too young to be in – love!" Vada answered, "And I was not too young to – marry you!"

The Duke smiled.

"That is, of course, true. At the same time our mothers arranged our marriage because they believed that we were suitable for each other."

"But we were not in love," Vada argued, "and, although I think you are a very nice kind person, I know now that I could never marry any man unless I was in love with him!"

She rose to stand beside the Duke.

"Please – please help me," she pleaded. "If you have ever loved anyone in your life, you will know what I am feeling. He is everything I have ever dreamt a man should be. I have always known that there was such a man somewhere in the world – if I could only find him!"

The anxiety in her voice and the passion in her words made the Duke look down at her.

Her face, eager and pleading, was upturned to his, and she looked very lovely.

"I will help you," he said quietly, "but I am not going to pretend that it is going to be easy."

"You will?" Vada cried. "Oh, thank you – *thank you*! I somehow felt –that you would understand."

The Duke gave a little sigh.

"I think that I am envious of you being so young and

so happy," he said. "Equally if you will leave everything to me I think I can promise you that you shall go back to Paris tomorrow and no one will try to prevent you."

"Do you mean that?" Vada asked. "Oh, thank you! Thank you from – the bottom of my heart!"

Impulsively, because she was so grateful, she bent forward and kissed the Duke on the cheek.

As she did so the door opened and the butler announced,

"Lord Peter, Your Grace!"

Vada moved from beside the Duke as he turned towards the door.

"Peter!" he exclaimed with an expression of pleasure in his voice, "I am so glad you came in answer to my telegram."

Indifferently Vada glanced towards the man walking across the library towards them.

She felt annoyed that he should interrupt them at this particular moment.

Then suddenly she was still – transfixed where she was standing!

It was *Pierre* who had come into the room!

Pierre, looking strange and very unlike himself in a frock coat that matched the Duke's, in a high white collar and an elegantly-tied cravat.

It was impossible not to recognise him, impossible not to feel that her heart had turned a double somersault within her breast!

"I came as quickly as I could," Pierre said.

"I knew you would," the Duke answered, "but I did not tell Mama that I had sent for you. So, if you will excuse me for a moment, I will just go and break the news to her before she hears it from the servants."

He turned towards Vada with a smile.

"I want you to meet my brother," he said. "Peter, this is Miss Emmeline Holtz, of whom you have heard."

As he spoke, the Duke left the library and the door closed behind him.

Vada and Pierre stood staring at each other.

She could not move.

Her voice had died in her throat.

"Miss – Emmeline – Holtz!" Pierre said slowly, a pause between each word. "So that is who you are!"

"I – can – I – was – " Vada began, only to be silenced as he interrupted,

"So you were deceiving me! So you were just enjoying yourself in Paris, intending all the time to come here and marry my brother for his title. It was what you set out to do, but you acted the part of the poor companion very cleverly!"

"Pierre – listen to me – " Vada begged, only to find that she could not make herself heard as Pierre went on, his voice growing louder,

"It was a splendid performance! Perfect! The innocent, young, unsophisticated Miss Sparling and I actually believed your plea of being frightened when I first took you to my studio!"

"I-I– can – explain – " Vada managed to gasp.

"Explain? What can you explain?" he asked. "That you were amusing yourself, as all Americans do when they come to Paris, without a thought of the consequences and without considering who might be hurt in the process?"

He laughed and it was not a pleasant sound.

"What a pity I did not leave you to enjoy the climax of

the Black Mass. You would have found it a great experience. Something else to add to your album of memories!"

His voice grew savage as he added,

"Perhaps, if they could have taken your soul from your body and replaced it with someone else's, it would have been a good thing. Wherever it had come from, it could not have been so low, so despicable, so pretentious as yours! The soul of a liar! The soul of a woman who is prepared to sell herself for a title!"

He almost spat the words to her and Vada put out her hands towards him, crying,

"Pierre – Pierre – you must listen – "

"I will listen to no more lies!" he said brutally.

Then his voice seemed to echo round the library as he added,

"Get out of my sight! I am going back to Paris and I hope to God that I never see you again!"

He walked away from her as he spoke towards the window.

He heard her give a little cry and then there was the sound of her footsteps running from the room.

Pierre stood at the window seeing nothing but the blackness of his own rage.

He was trembling with fury and there was a white line round his mouth.

How long he stood there with his fingers clenched he did not know, but he heard someone come into the room and knew that it was his brother.

"Mama is always unpredictable," the Duke said. "Now you have arrived, she is absolutely delighted and longing to see you. But first I want to talk to you, Peter."

Almost reluctantly, Pierre turned from the window and walked towards the mantelpiece.

The Duke did not seem to notice the expression on his face.

"I asked you to come home at once," he said, "because I want to tell you that I have made over The Castle and all the estates to you."

"You have done – what?" Pierre ejaculated.

"I was afraid that it would be rather a shock," the Duke said, "but there is nothing else I can do and only you can help."

"What are you talking about? What has happened?" Pierre enquired.

"I have known for some time that I have not been well," his brother replied. "Three days ago I went to see a specialist in London. What he told me confirms what I suspected."

"What is the matter with you?" Pierre asked.

"I have tuberculosis," the Duke answered. "If I go to Switzerland immediately and stay there I may live for a year or two, but it is unlikely that it will be much longer."

There was a silence.

Then Pierre put out his hand and laid it on his brother's arm.

"David – I cannot believe it!" he said and his voice was deeply moved.

"It's true," the Duke said, "and quite frankly, Peter, I don't mind very much. Everything has got on top of me this last year or so. There has been so much to do on the estate and no money to do it with. Mama has been difficult and I was beginning to feel that I could not carry on."

He sighed.

"As I told you in my letter, it was her idea entirely that I should marry this American girl. She fixed it all up and never even told me that the girl had agreed until she was on her way from America."

Pierre was very still and then he said in a voice that somehow sounded strange,

"I imagine from what I saw when I came into the room that you have told Miss Holtz about this and she has accepted the situation?"

The Duke smiled.

"I, of course, intended to tell her the truth, but there was no need."

"Why not?"

"Because the attractive Miss Holtz is madly in love with a man she has met in Paris! She has told me that she will not marry me and has persuaded me to help her to return there tomorrow."

"She told you that?"

Pierre's voice was hoarse.

"God knows if I am doing the right thing," the Duke said, "but she appears to be very much in love."

Pierre reached out and clutched his brother's arm.

"Tell me, David," he said, "in which room is Miss Holtz sleeping?"

The Duke looked at him in astonishment.

"Why should you want to know?" he asked.

"I will explain later," Pierre replied. "Just tell, where is she?"

"In the Queen's room of course. You might have guessed that Mama – "

The Duke found that he was talking to the air.

With incredible swiftness his brother had left the

library and was running across the hall.

The Duke looked after him in perplexity.

He could not imagine what was happening.

Pierre opened the door of the Queen's room without knocking and entered.

As he had expected, Vada was lying full length on the bed, crying.

Pierre closed the door behind him and locked it.

Then he walked across the room to look down at her.

He knew from the movement of her shoulders that her tears were a tempest.

"Vada!" he said in his deep voice.

"Go away!" she sobbed. "Go – away! I knew – you would – feel like – this!"

There was a note of utter despair in her voice, but the expression on Pierre's face was very tender.

He sat down on the bed with his shoulders against the pillows, exactly as he had done in the studio and pulled her gently into his arms.

She did not resist him, but went on crying against him.

"Why did you not tell me?" he asked after a moment.

"Mama said – no one would – ever – love me for – myself."

"When were you going to tell me?"

There was silence.

"You would have had to have told me sometime," he went on. "When did you think would be the proper moment?"

Vada raised her face from his shoulder.

The tears were running down her cheeks, her eyelashes were wet with them. Her mouth was soft and blurred, her lips were trembling as she pleaded,

"Please – marry me – Pierre. Please – *please*! We can give the – money away! You can forget it! But please – marry me. I cannot – live without you!"

There was a frantic note in her voice.

As her eyes searched his face and did not find the response she was seeking, she hid her face against him and she began to cry again.

"There are quite a number of things for us to discuss," Pierre said quietly.

There was a pause before Vada asked in a frightened voice,

"What are – they?"

"Let's start with an explanation as to why you came here," Pierre said.

"I felt I could not – marry you while – I was supposed to be – engaged to – another man," Vada stammered.

"And you were coming back to Paris to me tomorrow, letting me still think that you were someone else?"

"Y-Yes."

"How old is Miss Sparling – the real Miss Sparling?"

"N-nearly sixty I think," Vada replied, "she fractured her leg at Cherbourg and she said that I should go on to Paris – alone to buy my trousseau and my gowns."

"I am sure that she did not expect you to go out alone with strange men?"

"You – did not seem – strange."

"That is a prevarication, and you know it!" he said sternly. "How could you have been so crazy as to dine alone with someone you knew nothing about and go back to his studio afterwards?"

Vada did not answer for a moment, and then she said,

"I did not – know artists – slept in their studios – I

~211~

thought that they only – worked there."

"That does not explain why you dined alone, not only with me but with the Marquis."

"It is because it was my only – chance while I was free to do what I – wanted to do."

Pierre did not speak, and she added tremulously,

"I – thought I was being – adventurous."

"Adventurous!" Pierre exclaimed. "It terrifies me to think of the trouble that you might have found yourself in."

"I was in – trouble, but you – saved me!"

"By an outside chance that might only happen once in a million times."

Vada thought that he sounded severe and, as if to take his mind off her misdeeds, she said,

"You were pretending to me too! You were not trying – to find out about Miss Holtz for a newspaper?"

"No. My brother wrote and told me a marriage had been arranged for him without his knowledge and that the girl was in Paris at the *Hotel Meurice.*"

"So you wanted to see what I was – like."

"I was told Miss Holtz had not arrived, but I found her very young, very lovely and very naughty companion!"

Vada gave a little inarticulate murmur before she said,

"You pretended to be French."

"I was not really pretending," Pierre replied. "As I have said before, we have a lot to learn about each other. Actually my name really is 'Valmont'."

He knew that she was listening curiously and he went on,

"It was my Godfather's name. He was the Duc de Valmont and he was the first person who made me interested in French art. I spent many of my school holidays in France and afterwards, instead of going to Oxford as my brother had done, I went to the Sorbonne."

"The Paris University," Vada murmured, as if explaining it to herself.

"I was there for three years spending all my free time with my Godfather with the result that I became not only bilingual but very French in my outlook and tastes."

Vada did not interrupt and Pierre continued,

"As you see, I don't look like David and we have very different ideas on life. When I came back to England, I was critical of the way the estates were run. I was also bored. I have never got on well with my mother and so I returned to Paris."

"To become a – Symbolist!"

"I began to write and, as I was living in the Latin Quarter, it was far easier to be a Frenchman than an Englishman. I used my two first names and wrote as 'Pierre Valmont'."

He smiled before he said,

"I have concrete evidence of my industry, because a book I have written on Symbolism is being published next month."

"Why did you not tell me?" Vada asked.

"I wanted it to be a surprise."

"I shall be very – proud and very excited – when I see it," she said in a low voice.

"I enjoyed my life in Paris," Pierre said, "but now it is over."

"What do you mean?" Vada asked in alarm.

"David has just told me that he is very ill. He would not have been able to marry you even if you had wished to do so, because he has tuberculosis. The doctors insist that he must live in Switzerland."

"Oh, no!" Vada exclaimed. "I am sorry – terribly sorry."

"So am I," Pierre said. "And it means that I have to take over the estates."

Vada was very still.

"You mean – you must leave Paris – and live in England?"

"Yes," he replied.

There was silence, and then she said in a broken little voice,

"Then – you don't – need me?"

"I have not said so."

"But it is – true – is it not? If you are to – live here in England – you don't want – a wife?"

Pierre smiled.

"As a matter of fact," he said, "I shall need a wife much more urgently than I needed one in Paris."

He paused and Vada held her breath.

"There is only one person," he continued, "I would consider marrying!"

Vada raised her head from his shoulders and there was a sudden radiance in her eyes as if someone had switched on a thousand lights.

"You mean – me?" she whispered almost beneath her breath.

"Someone has to look after you," he said almost angrily. "You behave so badly, taking such inexpressible risks, that I cannot allow it to continue!"

"So you will marry me? You really will – marry me, Pierre? Please – say so!"

~214~

He pulled her roughly against him and his lips were on hers.

His kiss was not gentle or tender, but fierce and demanding. She felt a flame rising within her and knew that he felt the same.

She could only cling to him oblivious of everything except that once again she was close to him in a golden world where there was only themselves.

His mouth became more insistent, more passionate.

Vada felt that her body was melting into his. It was as if he drew her heart and her soul from between her lips and made them his.

At last Pierre raised his head and said in a voice that was curiously unsteady,

"You are so absurdly lovely, my darling, and I am not going to risk losing you. You will marry me as soon as possible."

"You – tried to be – sensible."

"And failed completely. Now I must have you as my wife."

He felt a quiver of ecstasy run through her.

"That is what I – long to be," she whispered, "and we can – throw away my horrible – money so that you will not – despise me because of it."

"It's much more difficult than that," Pierre replied. "You cannot evade your responsibilities, any more than I can evade mine."

"What do – you mean?"

"I mean that, just as I have to take over the estates and do my best for them, so you have to do what is right with your money."

"What is – right?" Vada asked in a frightened voice.

"There is a great deal to be done that requires money," Pierre answered. "The Grantham estate is like a huge hungry monster that devours everything it is given and always wants more."

He gave a sigh as if what he said depressed him, before he went on,

"There are the innumerable pensioners to be provided for, schools, alms houses and orphanages to be built. We also own a vast slum area in London where I am determined that the streets of crumbling houses shall be demolished and new ones built."

His voice was very serious as he continued,

"If you marry me, that is the way you are going to spend your millions. You will not be at parties in Worth gowns, glittering with diamonds, but you will be working as I shall work, to sweep away the abuses of an old *régime* and put something new and worthwhile in its place."

Vada gave a little cry.

"I can do – that with – you?"

"If you wish to," he answered, "because that is what I shall ask of my wife."

His arms tightened for a moment at the word and then he said,

"It's not going to be easy. There will be a great number of problems, a great number of headaches and perhaps a lot of opposition before I get what I want! Are you prepared to help me, my precious?"

"You know that all I – want is to be with – you," Vada replied passionately, "to do what you want me to do – to love – you."

She ceased speaking for a moment and then she said in a small voice,

"I thought that I was going to live with you in your studio – to cook and clean for you."

Pierre gave a little laugh.

"Perhaps we had better keep the studio. When you get too grand and puffed-up with your own importance, I will take you to Paris. We might even spend our honeymoon there."

Vada raised her face again.

"Alone?" she questioned.

"I was not thinking of asking anyone else to accompany us," Pierre replied with a hint of laughter in his voice.

"You know what I mean," Vada murmured.

"We will be alone, my darling," he said. "No lady's maids, no valets, no supercilious servants! In Paris there is only one old woman who comes in to scrub the floor!"

"I will look – after you," Vada whispered.

Pierre smiled.

"You will be able to show me how you can be a competent wife to a poor writer."

Vada's eyes were like stars before she said a little incoherently,

"I – don't – cook very well."

"But I do," Pierre answered, "so I will teach you."

"That will be wonderful! More wonderful than anything – that has ever happened to me. When can we be – married?"

Pierre drew her very close. His lips were on her hair before he said,

"That is another thing. I have no intention of going to New York to have the type of wedding your mother would expect. We are going to be married at once, very quietly, because I want David to be my best man, and the sooner he gets to Switzerland, the longer he will live."

"Mama will be angry – but nothing will matter if I am your wife."

"She will doubtless be consoled by the knowledge that her daughter will be a Duchess one day," Pierre said.

There was a touch of irony in his voice and then he continued,

"Leave your mother to me. I have my own mother to cope with as well. They had no right, either of them, to force you into a marriage with a man you had never seen."

"Your brother is – so kind."

"Was that your reason for kissing him?"

"I was thanking him!"

"I hope in future," Pierre said, "you will not show your gratitude so generously. It made me believe that you had promised to marry him, it also made me say some cruel things to you."

Vada hid her face again.

"How could you – think I was – like that?"

"I was counting the minutes until I would see you again. And then I thought that you had deceived me! "

"You knew – I – loved you."

"I believed you did. But, when I saw you kissing my brother, I thought I had been mistaken."

"I could never – never love – anyone but– you."

The emotion in Vada's voice was very moving.

"Will you forgive me?" Pierre asked softly.

"I will forgive you – anything as long as you will – marry me."

Pierre laughed tenderly.

"Like all women, you have a one-track mind. At the

same time, strangely enough, my lovely one, my mind wants the same thing. That we should be married and very quickly!"

He put his hand under her small chin and turned her face up to his. He had never seen a woman look so radiantly happy.

"We neither of us want to wait," he said gently. "We know that we belong to each other, we know that we have found what we have both been seeking since the beginning of time."

He felt her quiver.

"It is love, my precious, *ma belle*. It is love, magic and inexplicable, and you, who are a part of all the beauty in the world, are mine."

His lips were on hers as he finished speaking.

Vada felt again the wonder and ecstasy that had been hers that first night when Pierre's kiss had been part of the river, the sky and *Notre Dame*.

Now they were even closer.

It seemed as if she had no identity apart from him. She was his now and for Eternity.

She knew that there would be difficulties ahead, but it did not matter as long as they were together.

'I love – you. I love you – so desperately!' she wanted to say, but his lips held hers captive.

"*Ma petite* – my precious love," he murmured hoarsely.

She could feel his heart beating frantically as the flame rising within them both became a fire.

A fire that would burn away all that was wrong, unpleasant and evil – a fire that was part of the Divine!

A fire that was lifting them both into the starlit sky where there was only the music and poetry of love.

OTHER BOOKS IN THIS SERIES

The Barbara Cartland Eternal Collection is the unique opportunity to collect all five hundred of the timeless beautiful romantic novels written by the world's most celebrated and enduring romantic author.

Named the Eternal Collection because Barbara's inspiring stories of pure love, just the same as love itself, the books will be published on the internet at the rate of four titles per month until all five hundred are available.

The Eternal Collection, classic pure romance available worldwide for all time.

1. Elizabethan Lover
2. The Little Pretender
3. A Ghost in Monte Carlo
4. A Duel of Hearts
5. The Saint and the Sinner
6. The Penniless Peer
7. The Proud Princess
8. The Dare-Devil Duke
9. Diona and a Dalmatian
10. A Shaft of Sunlight
11. Lies for Love
12. Love and Lucia
13. Love and the Loathsome Leopard
14. Beauty or Brains
15. The Temptation of Torilla
16. The Goddess and the Gaiety Girl
17. Fragrant Flower
18. Look, Listen and Love
19. The Duke and the Preacher's Daughter
20. A Kiss For The King
21. The Mysterious Maid-Servant
22. Lucky Logan Finds Love
23. The Wings of Ecstasy
24. Mission to Monte Carlo
25. Revenge of the Heart
26. The Unbreakable Spell
27. Never Laugh at Love
28. Bride to a Brigand
29. Lucifer and the Angel
30. Journey to a Star
31. Solita and the Spies
32. The Chieftain without a Heart
33. No Escape from Love
34. Dollars for the Duke
35. Pure and Untouched
36. Secrets
37. Fire in the Blood
38. Love, Lies and Marriage
39. The Ghost who fell in love
40. Hungry for Love
41. The wild cry of love
42. The blue eyed witch
43. The Punishment of a Vixen
44. The Secret of the Glen
45. Bride to The King
46. For All Eternity
47. A King in Love
48. A Marriage Made in Heaven
49. Who Can Deny Love?
50. Riding to The Moon
51. Wish for Love

52. Dancing on a Rainbow
53. Gypsy Magic
54. Love in the Clouds
55. Count the Stars
56. White Lilac
57. Too Precious to Lose
58. The Devil Defeated
59. An Angel Runs Away
60. The Duchess Disappeared
61. The Pretty Horse-breakers
62. The Prisoner of Love
63. Ola and the Sea Wolf
64. The Castle made for Love
65. A Heart is Stolen
66. The Love Pirate
67. As Eagles Fly
68. The Magic of Love
69. Love Leaves at Midnight
70. A Witch's Spell
71. Love Comes West
72. The Impetuous Duchess
73. A Tangled Web
74. Love Lifts the Curse
75. Saved By A Saint
76. Love is Dangerous
77. The Poor Governess
78. The Peril and the Prince
79. A Very Unusual Wife
80. Say Yes Samantha
81. Punished with love
82. A Royal Rebuke
83. The Husband Hunters
84. Signpost To Love
85. Love Forbidden
86. Gift of the Gods
87. The Outrageous Lady
88. The Slaves of Love
89. The Disgraceful Duke
90. The Unwanted Wedding
91. Lord Ravenscar's Revenge
92. From Hate to Love
93. A Very Naughty Angel
94. The Innocent Imposter
95. A Rebel Princess
96. A Wish Come True
97. Haunted
98. Passions In The Sand

99. Little White Doves of Love
100. A Portrait of Love
101. The Enchanted Waltz
102. Alone and Afraid
103. The Call of the Highlands
104. The Glittering Lights
105. An Angel in Hell
106. Only a Dream
107. A Nightingale Sang
108. Pride and the Poor Princess
109. Stars in my Heart
110. The Fire of Love
111. A Dream from the Night
112. Sweet Enchantress
113. The Kiss of the Devil
114. Fascination in France
115. Love Runs in
116. Lost Enchantment
117. Love is Innocent
118. The Love Trap
119. No Darkness for Love
120. Kiss from a Stranger
121. The Flame Is Love
122. A Touch Of Love
123. The Dangerous Dandy
124. In Love In Lucca

Made in United States
North Haven, CT
09 December 2023